Amora

Amora

Stories

NATALIA BORGES POLESSO

Translated by Julia Sanches

AMAZON **CROSSING**

Text copyright © 2015 by Natalia Borges Polesso
Translation copyright © 2020 by Julia Sanches
All rights reserved.

Previously published as *Amora* by Não Editora in Brazil in 2015. Translated from the Portuguese by Julia Sanches. First published in English by Amazon Crossing in 2020.

Published by Amazon Crossing, Seattle

www.apub.com

Amazon, the Amazon logo, and Amazon Crossing are trademarks of Amazon.com, Inc., or its affiliates.

ISBN-13: 9781542019774 (hardcover)
ISBN-10: 154201977X (hardcover)

ISBN-13: 9781542004336 (paperback)
ISBN-10: 1542004330 (paperback)

Cover design by David Drummond

Printed in the United States of America

First edition

To amores and amoras

Contents

BIG & JUICY

FIRST TIMES

She was done with the whole virgin thing. At seventeen, it was a sin. She was tired of lying to her friends about her first time. Tired. She'd forgotten the true parts in the lie she'd told and kept tacking on random facts. He had a Chevette. Played 4 Non Blondes. My panties were green. We ate fries. He doesn't live in the area. Green panties? Who wears green panties when they know they're going to put out? None of it was real. She wasn't a *songamonga* who'd never done anything, but she was still a virgin. She was tired.

She was a junior in the evening session at an ordinary public high school where on Fridays people ordinarily skipped out after second period. Not even the teachers showed up for the last two. The administration had already cut Fridays to four periods and even that hadn't helped. There were three bars around school: 1) a weird joint where god-awful bands played equally god-awful covers on off-key instruments; people drank catuaba, because it was what they had and it was cheap—catuaba-and-grape-Fanta mixers were officially the hot new thing—and there was no question that was where this generation's livers would start rotting; 2) the skater bar where they sold beers at reasonable prices and every shade of Bols liqueurs, where illegal drugs were consumed in plain sight, most of all weed—not her, she still wasn't into illegal drugs; 3) the gas station convenience store where people could buy a quart of rotgut vodka and Coke and enjoy the facilities, read: covered area, grimy bathroom, small brick wall behind the car wash. End result: jam-packed bars, empty school.

Friday, 7:25 p.m., the first bell rang and half her classmates walked into the room. The other half waved at her to follow them to the back of the school. One of the guys lifted the chain-link fence and everyone crawled through. There'd be no going to class that Friday. Everybody headed for bar number two. She followed. Everybody walked in, everybody sat down, everybody drank, everybody got up to dance. Like a shoal, never parting. Until a friend tugged her by the hand to go for a smoke. She didn't smoke. She didn't like cigarettes. She thought of how her dad, a smoker, had never smoked a single cigarette in their house. She lit it. Took two puffs and was interrupted by a very deep voice telling her that that's not how you smoke. It really wasn't. The voice belonged to Luís Augusto Marcelo Dias Prado. That was how he introduced himself. Luís Augusto Marcelo Dias Prado. His name was like too many building blocks snapped end on end, on the verge of breaking. It wasn't a good name. Three Fridays later they were dating. Her feelings for him were inversely proportional to her physics grade. She was bad at physics. She was good at liking him. That was one thing she had, at least. Two, even: the lie about her nonvirginity and the unmentionable thing.

Eight Fridays before the Friday she met Luís Augusto Marcelo Dias Prado, she had been with Letícia, her smoker friend, sitting tipsy on a sofa in her house gossiping about Mandala, the junior-year dyke; and then about where she performed; and then about maybe going there sometime; then about the sudden onslaught of lesbians in that telenovela set in the shopping mall; then about how totally weird the world was; and then about how they couldn't really control those sorts of feelings; and then about how she wanted to kiss Letícia's red lips; and then about how Letícia would like that too, so long as Vitor was with them; and then about how she had to study some more for her physics exam. That interaction planted itself in her everyday feelings. Letícia's red lips. Thoughts that had for years been trapped in some shadowy part of her head, now released in words. Words that had ended up in Letícia's head. She'd never confessed any of that to anyone, and in all the Fridays that followed until the day she went over to Luís Augusto Marcelo Dias Prado's house, it seemed like she'd never confessed it at all.

He didn't have a car. 4 Non Blondes wasn't playing on the radio. Her panties were burgundy. They didn't eat fries. She didn't even have time to take her bra off. Everything was already over. She decided that everything before had been way better than during. Then she went to the bathroom and saw that her face was still as virginal as ever. Black hair tucked behind ears, no makeup, shoulders so skinny they were pointy, a touch of blood between her thighs. She left the bathroom liking physics much more than she used to and asked to leave. Luís Augusto Marcelo Dias Prado didn't understand. He was a good person, despite his name. He even wanted to go out with her. Her mom loved when he called the house in that deep voice she still couldn't put a face to but already pictured at Sunday lunches. It never happened. She started avoiding him and started going to class on Fridays. She didn't pick up the phone and asked her mom to lie and tell the handsomest voice in town that she wasn't home.

On the Saturday following the Friday she'd gone to his house, she called Letícia. She told her about the previous day and how she'd lied about her first time and how she wished there hadn't been an onslaught of lesbians at the shopping mall and how she had weird dreams that involved Linda Perry and about wanting to kiss Letícia's red lips that day on the sofa. Letícia, for her part, told her that first times were always like that and maybe she hadn't done it right, maybe she'd been nervous and should try again. She said nothing about lesbians, telenovelas, or Linda Perry, and nothing about kisses on red lips.

She only got up the courage to go to school on Wednesday. She couldn't look Letícia in the eye, and she didn't have to, because on Wednesday Letícia was the one who didn't show up. On Thursday, everything seemed far away, because that's how life works at seventeen, when time's elastic and changes according to your mood and those innocent needs. Time was lovely on Thursdays, at seventeen. And they met. She said absolutely nothing about the phone call, neither did Letícia. Half their grade was planning a party at some guy's house, so no one was going to school the next day. She went straight to the address. A car dealership. She rang the bell, a classmate answered. Through the pale smoke she spotted Letícia sitting on a wicker chair beside the grill. Glass in hand. Blue Curaçao with Sprite. Back then, Curaçao and Sprite was infinitely superior to catuaba with grape Fanta or vodka and Coke mixed in a plastic bottle; these days, they're on a par.

Everybody walked in, everybody sat down, everybody drank, everybody ate, everybody drank again, everybody got up to dance, everybody drank some more. Like a shoal, never parting. Until Letícia tugged her by the hand to smoke. She shuffled her feet through the gravel while Letícia searched her jacket pockets for a pack of menthols. Letícia shook something in front of her eyes. It was a key. The key chain said *Moss Green Voyage*. They found it. Letícia opened the door and climbed into the back seat. She followed, trying not to pin her hopes on something that might not be mutual. They didn't have a car, weren't old enough to drive. There was no radio in the Voyage and no 4 Non Blondes. Letícia's panties were lacy and purple, hers were gray, the cotton fabric frayed to the limit of decency. Neither of them had time to take off their bras. It was clumsy, like first times usually are. Full of knocking teeth and jerky movements.

They heard Vitor yelling that Moisés was chugging a quart of *butiá* cachaça. They got out of the car and caught Rodrigo and Bruna behind a Fiat Tempra, respectively hiking up pants and pulling down tops. No one saw anything or said anything. Not even them. Letícia kept on going out with Vitor until the end of the year. Their group kept on cutting Friday classes. And she passed physics.

EDUARDA, DO NOT PASS OUT

It's one of those things that happens, you fall. No. You splat on the ground. You fear being the object of ridicule and lie still, slumped. The cases scatter, the blue folder made of God knows what about to explode, your head about to explode, a war about to explode. You get up, get on the bus, life proceeds in jolts. You were born to the right family, which meets at your grandma's every Sunday, outside town. Although you don't even feel obligated to go anymore, you do, because you always have, your whole life. Your mom, grandma, aunts. Suddenly, you realize there are no men around the table, no men in the house, no men within a five-kilometer radius. The store where you and your boozy aunts buy beer, cachaça, and a leg of artisanal salami is five kilometers away. You wonder what artisanal salami is. You taste the salami and don't make out any artisanal flavors, only canker sores; your aunts suggest arnica cachaça, because it kills them off. Until then you thought arnica was for muscle pain. You take a sip of cachaça, your life becomes hot like an infernal summer afternoon on that nearly deserted beach you've gone to every break for the last eighteen years. Your aunts laugh. You go back home. You lie in bed, kind of nauseated, wondering how that bruise on your thigh managed to triple in size in a matter of days.

And you remember.

One of those things that happens, Laura and Mauro at the end of the hallway, by the window, chatting like they were super close. Laura touching Mauro's arm with her hand, him laughing. The folder was really heavy, leading me to assume I'd have a lot of work that afternoon and, probably, the entire weekend. I walked down the stairs cursing Laura in my head—she really was a slut. She'd broken up with me the week before, and now there she was chitchatting with Mauro, the criminal law professor. I'd gone through the bother of helping her, writing up summaries, moving my shifts around so I could study with the bald-faced skank, and what for? For her to kick my ass out the door and get straight to it, a hard, perfectly aimed kick, right smack in the ass, *trouxa*. I've never been good at swearing. I walked down the first flight of stairs and considered getting a cup of hot tea, the thought a comfort. Reaching the first landing, I heard a voice calling my name, looked up and saw Tábata. Hi, Eduarda! Don't work too hard, hey? Have a nice weekend. Hi, Tábata. Sure thing, bye. I extended my leg, which was poised for the next step, and that's when it happened. Tensed knee, the sole of my foot ready to meet the firmness of a floor that wasn't there. Then, the second that precedes the calamity, when I think to myself that I shouldn't have done that thing I did. And the fall. Me, down there, strewed, the papers still fluttering around me. I spent five, ten seconds wondering if I was alive, if I was all right, if it was worth getting up off the floor. The people in the classroom opposite the staircase all rushed toward me, followed by an avalanche of voices. Are you all right? Oh my God! Don't move. Can you move? Grab her stuff, guys? There's paper back there. Was that all you were carrying? What happened? Step away, folks, let her breathe. I blinked sort of slowly, I think, and, when I opened my eyes, saw Laura's worried face hovering above mine. Eduarda, are you all right? What happened? I lifted a single foot. I'm all right, guys, I'm all right. Thanks, hand the folder here. I've gotta go. Have a nice weekend.

On the street, I took a deep breath and felt my ribs groan. I pressed them with my fingers. Nothing was broken, but my leg was killing me. I walked to the bus stop, dragging one foot behind me. It wasn't long before the bus arrived. I set the folder in my lap and took out my cell. Hey, Mom. Hi. I fell, I'm all right, though. On my way home. Eduarda, sweetie? What do you mean, you fell? Where? Down some stairs. What do you mean, Eduarda? What stairs? The stairs in the college building.

What sort of stairs? What're they made of? What do you mean, Mom? The staircase is metal, wood, stone, it has yellow antislip treads, sort of rubbery steps. But Eduarda, were the steps in one piece? They weren't coming up, were they? Had you been drinking? No, Mom. No what, Eduarda, the steps weren't in one piece or you hadn't been drinking? No drinking. So how come you fell, Eduarda? Mom, I'm nearly there, we'll talk in a bit.

In the elevator, I started to regret having mentioned the fall at all, and as the apartment door opened, I knew I'd made the wrong decision. Eduarda, what've you done to your hair? I looked at the mirror and noticed that my hair tie had shifted left and sat in a sort of half-undone ponytail, that I looked like a cross between Punky Brewster and Elvira, Mistress of the Dark. Eduarda, you're all banged up! I had a tear in my shirt and another in my pants, but I wasn't all banged up. Mom, I'm not feeling well. Did you hit your head, Eduarda? Mom, I fell down some stairs, I must've hit my head at least three times. Eduarda, we've got to go to the hospital right now! How come they didn't call an ambulance, Eduarda? Or SAMU! Mom, I just want to get out of these pants and lie down for a bit.

I pulled down one pant leg. A bruise the size of an open hand gleamed in the reflection of the narcissistic and probative living room mirror. I gave it a deep prod and felt a nauseating pain. Mom, I'm not feeling well. Lie down, Eduarda, lie down right there on the couch. I wanted to ask for a glass of water, but my voice wouldn't come out, my vision clouded, I began to sweat. EDUARDA? EDUARDA? YOU'RE WHITE AS A SHEET. DO NOT PASS OUT, EDUARDA. I'M GOING TO GRAB YOU A GLASS OF WATER, DO YOU WANT SOME WATER, EDUARDA? EDUARDA? WOULD YOU LIKE SOME WATER? I would've passed out if it weren't for my mom's voice piercing my eardrums like a needle. I felt an intense urge to laugh, but the pain was overwhelming. I thought of Laura and Mauro at the end of the hallway. What might've been a laugh turned into hiccupy tears, the kind that gush out of a scrunched-up face, creased in pain. But I had no voice, only hiccups and weakness; I wished I'd died, face-planted, broken my neck and every tooth, bitten off my tongue, been paralyzed. EDUARDA? My mom fanned me with an issue of *National Geographic*. The one with the noseless Afghan girl. The Taliban had cut her nose off as a warning for her not to try and leave her family again. I wished I were married to Laura, or Mauro, I don't know. I just wanted to leave home. It would've been easier, I think, with one of them. Eduarda, your color's coming back. I glanced at my reflection in the hallway mirror, saw my mouth hooked in a silent cry, and righted it again. It was just pain. Physical, emotional. Eduarda, are you all right? I'm taking you to the hospital, right this instant. It's all right, Mom. I just want a glass of water is all. A glass of water? Why didn't you say so earlier, Eduarda? Did you really have to make such a big fuss about it? I thought I might die seeing you in that state—and all you want is a glass of water? Yeah, Mom, a glass of water, and some Rivotril. All I have is diazepam. That'll do, Mom. And she stomped out the door in her puppy slippers. EDUARDA, we're out of diazepam! All I've got is alprazolam, but it'll help you relax, you want some? Yeah. I'm going to take one too 'cause you nearly scared the living daylights out of me, look, feel my heart, it's beating up my throat, you nearly murdered me. Here you go, don't you want to eat something first? No, Mom, I just want to sleep, that's all. Tomorrow we're off to your gram's. Yeah, I know. How do you know? 'Cause we always go, Mom. Course we always go, she's your grandma. You might not appreciate her right now, but you'll miss her once she's gone. We'll go tomorrow and come back Sunday evening. Do you think you'll be able to drive, Eduarda? I'm not sure, Mom. I'll see how I feel in the morning. You taking all that junk with you, Eduarda? You won't have time to talk to your aunts if all you do is work and study. You never think of your family. You may think you're totally self-sufficient, but you're not. Mom, I've just got a few things to finish up. There'll be time to spend with you, too, don't worry. I'm not worried, Eduarda, I'm just giving you some advice, you know. Then you start falling all over the place and you don't know why. In that moment, I didn't know if my mom was talking nonsense or if the drugs were having an effect. You planning to sleep on the couch, Eduarda? No. I got up, walked to my room, dragging behind me my pants, still wrapped around one of my ankles, and lay down.

Eduarda, it's eleven, c'mon now. Let's get up, hit the road. Grandma already called. All right, Mom, let's go. That friend of yours, Laura, called too. Ice ran down my back and my legs buckled. I gripped the doorframe. What'd she want? To know how you're doing, *ora*, and Eduarda, I asked her how you fell, and she said she hadn't seen it herself but that your classmates said it wasn't pretty. Sounds like you flew over the three first steps, then rolled all the way down to the bottom. No one knows how you managed not to break anything or crack your neck. The ice melted in a blaze of rage and shame.

Grandma lives in a quiet place, in a neighborhood with a faux-rustic air. It doesn't need much, to be honest, the town's already pretty rural, but its function as a country home makes the thirty-minute drive worthwhile. There's a vegetable garden, fruit trees that my aunts refer to as an orchard, dogs, cats, and a woodstove. My aunts were planting herbs in the garden, and I went to help. My hands were stained with the scent of basil and rosemary. Eduarda, let's go to the shop after lunch and get a drink to lift your spirits. Of course. Your mom said you fell down the stairs. Yeah, I did. You in pain, hon? Not much, my leg's just a bit bruised up is all. Look after yourself, kid, you've always got your head in the clouds. Yeah, I'll look after myself, Tia. I'm the most grounded person in our family, I'm just the one with the rottenest luck, I almost said but didn't. Rose is coming over for lunch on Sunday. That's great, Tia.

Mom has three sisters, Marga, Rose, and Deise, who was adopted and is younger than me. When my grandpa passed away, Grandma adopted Aunt Deise from a couple who couldn't look after their kid. Grandma never mourned him and to this day pretends nothing happened. None of my aunts are married. Marga and Deise live with Grandma. Rose lives in another town, for work, and Mom lives in the center of town, on my account, she says. It was easier for me to go to school that way. Grandpa and Dad died in the same car accident. Mom doesn't talk about it, either. I've never asked. And that's what we're like, we don't ask much. I'm not sure if the topic is forbidden, or if we just act like this because it's the way things are. Eduarda! There's a car here, a friend of yours.

It was Laura, reversing over my grandma's hydrangeas. I said nothing and kept my face set in its I'm-just-planting-some-basil expression. I came to see how you were doing. I'm all right, Laura, you and Mauro doing okay, too? What're you talking about, Eduarda? I'm talking about the fact that I saw you guys having a little chat in the hallway on Friday. Are you denying it? Laura looked at me incredulously, then started to slowly open her mouth. Laura, please don't deny it, you're a terrible liar, it isn't pretty. Eduarda, I was just telling Mauro I did well on his test thanks to you. Eduarda, are you totally insane? We were talking about you. I was telling him I wanted to get back together with you, and he said he thought it was a great idea. I came here because he told me to come, but I'm not so sure it was such a good idea after all. Please, Laura, stop. Eduarda, I called you yesterday and this morning and your mom said you were resting, but the truth is I've wanted to talk to you since Tuesday and it's like you're avoiding me. Don't be ridiculous, Laura. What do you mean? All right, all right. You said what you came to say, now beat it. Laura glared at me resentfully and started walking to her car while my mom hollered, EDUARDA, IS YOUR FRIEND NOT STAYING FOR LUNCH?

By Saturday afternoon, my mouth was covered in canker sores. Grandma has a gift for making the most acidic tomato sauces in the world. Whenever she makes spaghetti with tomato sauce, my mouth is almost instantly covered in ulcers. I spent all afternoon and night reading up on court cases and biting the raised skin around the sores. I knew I'd have to spend time with the family on Sunday.

I didn't sleep, got up off the armchair, and went for coffee in the kitchen. Grandma was already prepping lunch. It was a tradition. Stuffing ourselves with food from the moment we arrived until the moment we left. Grandma, don't you get tired of cooking? What else can I do, honey? I like cooking, it passes the time, and life, and at least we're eating, and you know, people talk less when their mouths are full. And when their tummies are full, they spend less time thinking about nonsense. You're too skinny, sweetie, you should eat more and think less. I don't talk much, do I, Grandma? You don't talk at all. Might do you good to talk a little more and not keep everything locked up inside: ideas all in a jumble, things seen and made up, it's no good at all. You're right, Grandma. She was right. Stuff I saw all mixed up with stuff I made up. Me acting like I was cool and composed, then tumbling down the stairs.

That afternoon at the shop, my aunts gave me some arnica cachaça to taste and asked if it was a guy I was upset over; my being so quiet, my face so blank, it could only be a man. It's not a guy. We know. And they split their sides laughing. I kept my face set in its I'm-just-planting-some-basil expression. I took a sip of that cachaça, then tried another, sweeter one. I ate a piece of salami that turned my stomach, then asked Mom to drive me home. Why, Eduarda? 'Cause I drank, Mom, this time I did have something to drink. Gosh, Eduarda, you'll kill me if you keep on like this. Go on then, hand me the keys.

You lie in bed, kind of nauseated, wondering how that bruise on your thigh managed to triple in size in a matter of days. You try to come up with an explanation for the bruise, the nausea, maybe even life. You probably overexerted your leg. You drove. You know you'll have to get out of bed to throw up, but at first you think of nothing. You're sleepy and contemplate choking on your own vomit. You know that when stuff gets mixed up like that in your head it's because you're tired. You're exhausted. The walls spin. You shut your eyes, take a deep breath, and think that one second you're up above, your thoughts steady on your shoulders, and then suddenly your legs are flying over your head.

GRANDMA, ARE YOU A LESBIAN?

Grandma Clarissa's cutlery fell on her plate, making the porcelain ding. My cousin Joaquin's jaw still hung open, his fork smacking against his lips as he waited for her answer. Beatriz echoed the word in question form: "What's a lesbian?" I stayed quiet. Joaquim knew, he was going to tell Grandma, and then the whole family, on me. A deathly heat climbed up my neck, making the area behind my ears hurt. I pictured the scene unfolding before me: *Grandma, are you a lesbian? Because Joana is.* Shame plastered on my face, betraying me before the betrayal. I squeezed my eyes shut and drew my chest in, waiting for the shot to fire. Behind my eyelids, Taís and I kissed in the last row of the humanities section of the college library. I opened my eyes again and dizzily saw my grandma, her gaze still low, Joaquim still smacking his lips with his fork, and Beatriz barely kicking her small legs on the chair.

Grandma Clarissa was a history teacher, which is why her house was crammed full of books, atlases, guides, VHS documentaries, magazines, papers, everything. As a kid, I'd ask her what was inside all those books, and she'd say stories, lots and lots of stories, about different people, places, and times, all of them told in different ways. She'd ask if I wanted to hear one, then tell me to pick a book. My eyes were aflame with curiosity. I'd run all over the house and stumble back with more books than I could carry, throw everything down on the sofa, and run back to fetch the one I'd lost on the way. Grandma would laugh heartily and say, Hold on a second, how many stories do you want me to tell you? I don't think we'll have time for all of these! My eyes shone greedily, waiting for her to begin. Which one do you want? I'd point to a random book. All right, then. And she'd begin: Ah, an excellent story! I'll never forget this one. It's about a man called Gregor Samsa, a salesman. After a night filled with troubled dreams, he wakes up feeling kind of strange, so strange he can't get out of bed. I'd felt like that before too, I thought. His mother goes to check on him, but he doesn't open the door. His sister goes to check on him, he still doesn't open the door. Even his boss decides to stop by his house—after all, Gregor had never been late to work. If my teacher came knocking at my door I'd better have an excellent excuse, I thought. So he forced the door open. Everybody was shocked. Gregor Samsa was a bug! A bug? Gosh! I said. Like a cockroach. A ribbon of drool hung from my mouth, forming a puddle on the sofa. *Metamorphosis* was one of the first books I ever read, not counting books for so-called kids. But I think that was only when I was eleven. I presented the book in my reading class, and even though I'd read it on my own and come to my own conclusions, I told it just the way my granny had when I was six, with all the suspense and discovery revealed at the right moments.

My parents worked a lot, so us kids always went to Grandma's after school. Grandma and Mom thought it was best to go to school in the mornings because that was when our brains were most alert. I've studied in the mornings ever since. These days, I find it weird that there are evening sessions at university. I get so drowsy—I can't control it—especially when the Latin professor, a little old man with a liturgical voice who runs on coffee and milk candy, gets talking. It was in his class that I met Taís.

I only noticed Taís halfway through the semester. She came in with her leg in a cast and sat next to me. I always sat by the door, right in the front. She thought she'd be more comfortable there. I offered to lend a hand. I've got a notebook, folder, coffee, plus my crutches, and no one to help out, she said, it's like I'm invisible. Taís studied linguistics; I studied literature. I'm glad Latin was required for both majors. During break, I asked if she wanted me to grab her another coffee. She said yes. We spent the rest of that class, the next one, and the one after talking, until one day she was absent. I hadn't asked for her contact details, not her phone or her email, I didn't even know her full name, nothing. I spent the whole week wondering if I'd see her again, if she'd died or dropped out, if some awful thing had happened.

The following week, when she came in smiling, without her cast, I asked why she'd been absent. She stretched her slender leg over the bench, wound her arm through mine, and gave me a lollipop in exchange for me helping her up a flight of stairs. During break, we went to the library. She said she needed a book. She couldn't remember its name but said she knew where it was, so we walked to the last row, which was windowless and dimly lit. It's back there, she said, tugging me by the hand to where the shelf almost touched the wall. She grabbed the book and peeked inside. Then she looked at me and with a quick hand pulled me by the jacket collar until I was right next to her. She touched her forehead to mine. I knew what to do, I'd just never done it. Taís smiled with her enormous white teeth, smiled right in my mouth.

After our nanny was fired on account of the incident with the woodstove and half the kitchen catching fire, we started spending afternoons with Grandma. With her and Aunt Carolina. Around three p.m., Grandma set the table for tea. Blue-flowered teacups, the porcelain set, silverware, a tray. A little after lunch, she went to the bakery, leaving us on our own, and came back twenty minutes later with a boxful of treats that never failed to spark our curiosity. Aunt Carolina arrived a little after three. Grandma became radiant.

Aunt Carolina nearly always had an embarrassed look in her eye—I remember now—an uncertain step, hands heavy with rings hooked on each other, shoulders always angled upward. She looked like she didn't want to be there. I remember because she was very beautiful and because I liked copying her. I was fascinated by how Aunt Carolina could have white hair yet not seem old.

Grandma always said we shouldn't bother them during teatime and filled our room with all sorts of things to keep us busy. On one of those afternoons, I grabbed some talcum powder, dumped it over my head, and went to the kitchen to show them my white hair. Aunt Carolina laughed and pulled me onto her lap. I remember asking how old she was and why she didn't look old even though she had white hair. My brother and I figured out a way to stay in the kitchen. But after that day, her visits became less frequent and Grandma got sad in a way that was painful to see. She went around the house crying and secretly smoked in a corner of the balcony. I think she might have been drinking, too, because during that time Grandma was downhearted and there were weird smells wafting around her. A whole winter and spring passed before Aunt Carolina started visiting again. I remember it clearly because it was Joaquim's birthday. It was like Grandma became a different person. She was well dressed, content, and smelled of perfume and lavender moisturizer again. Things are starting to make sense now, fifteen years later. Grandma really is a lesbian.

"Joaquim, are you done with your food?" she asked.

"No."

"And where did you hear that I'm a lesbian?"

"I overheard Mom and Dad talking."

"Ah."

My hands froze and however much I tried to chew, the food just wouldn't go down. I got up from the table and walked to the sink, feigning disinterest.

"Joana?" Grandma said.

"Yeah?" I answered in my quietest voice.

"Pass the pepper."

"Sure, Grandma."

I took the pepper grinder to the table and was about to run off when she said: "Aren't you going to sit down so you can hear what I have to say to your cousin?"

I sat. Actually, I had sat without even realizing, as if automatically. My mind was unsettled, the dots finally connecting.

"Yes," I said.

Joaquim started laughing and Beatriz laughed with him.

"Joana, is there something you'd like to ask me?"

"Is Aunt Carolina coming today?" The question had come out all wrong, but even so Grandma understood.

"Yes, she's coming. She's coming today. And tomorrow. She comes here every day, which you've known since you were little. Is there anything else you'd like to ask?"

"No."

"Are you sure?"

I shook my head no but muttered a yes slurred with curiosity. Grandma started telling the whole story, and she was really good at telling stories. As she spoke, I stared at a tapestry that took up the entire wall behind her, a medieval-themed tapestry, a village fair. Two details have always caught my attention: the drunk dwarf and, a bit farther back, two women dancing behind a tree. As I stared at the tapestry, Taís pervaded my thoughts. I thought of her warm hands on my body, under my jacket, and then of Aunt Carolina's ringed hands touching Grandma's body. On the tapestry, two women held hands. I breathed heavily and Taís came back. I stuck my face in her hair and took a deep breath at the nape of her neck. But pulling away, I saw Aunt Carolina's white hair over Grandma Clarissa's face. In another section of the tapestry, a pint of beer was poured over a yellow woolen floor, Taís and I danced in her room and after one or two spins turned into Aunt Carolina and Grandma Clarissa, who fell breathless on the bed. I felt like I'd missed a huge part of the story. In the end, Grandma was saying, Twenty years, it's been twenty years. Joaquim asked why she and Aunt Carolina didn't live together. Grandma didn't answer that one. She said that's enough stories for today and then said they didn't live together because they didn't want to. But then I remembered Aunt Carolina had been married to Mr. Carlos. It occurred to me that maybe she couldn't be with Grandma. It occurred to me that maybe they'd never once danced or gone drinking together—or maybe they had. I thought of how naturally Taís and I went about things. I thought of how scared I was to tell my family, and of all the teachers and classmates who already knew about us. I closed my eyes and saw Grandma's and Aunt Carolina's mouths touching, in spite of every obstacle. I wanted to know more, I wanted to know everything, but I couldn't bring myself to ask.

WILD INSIDE

I turned the key in the keyhole, and as the door opened, my whole world turned with it. The mood on the apartment walls was the same. The color was ice and we'd chosen it because it was easy to match to other color blocks, which we never did. I walked to the end of the hall and stopped at the doorway to the room on the right. She wasn't there. I dropped my backpack and walked heavily back to the kitchen over the loose parquet. Nothing. Not in the living room, not in the bathroom, nor the study. I walked to the balcony and opened the rackety wood blinds. Empty, and in the bright morning light, the apartment seemed much larger than I remembered.

When Luiza left, leaving me with the bills to pay, I had to move out. I threw up for three days straight. Out of anger and fear. Fear of being alone. I only found out Luiza had fled our home because, following a weeklong quarrel, I decided to call. I called her cell, no answer. I called again and she was out of range. I called her workplace and they told me that she'd moved to Rio de Janeiro. I don't remember much about that time, except throwing up and crying for days, and that everything was fuzzy, horizontal. I moved out of the apartment because nowhere in my life plans—which had until then been ours—was it written that I would have to pay the bills on my own or decide by myself on a color to melt the ice encrusted in the walls around me.

I left and moved into the apartment of a friend who was going away on an exchange. She handed me the key and told me I could stay, but could I do her this one favor, could I change the kitchen faucet, or the little rubber thing on the faucet—it was on the fritz—then left. I stayed. It was a nice apartment, unfamiliar and completely quiet. I went back to Caetano.

"You're not in control."

Every time I ended up in his armchair, I felt like burrowing into its mossy velvet, like I was lichenizing—melding with the fabric's fur until I'd dissolved into its green, lifeless embrace. The rug between us was a black hole. A spiral drawing that sucked up my eyes and thoughts. I sat there in silence, staring at the curtain over the window behind him. I wanted to stay just like that, hardly taking in the hot January air. But the hole yanked my eyes to the middle of the room, and next thing I knew, there he was, eyes fixed on me as he waited for me to pour out my insides. As if it were easy, or effortless, or ordinary to draw our tensions to the surface. To make words breach our throats and come out nice and neat, full of exact or ambiguous meaning. I really did try to organize myself beforehand, to tidy up my thoughts before speaking, before opening my mouth. I'd spend the entire week rehearsing my part of the act, my part of the dialogue. But when Caetano opened the door, my thoughts were sucked into the bottomless vacuum of that room where everything seemed out to hurt me. Everything I said came out muddled. Not only thoughts came to the surface, but also, mixed in with my words, a load of clustering and stuttering that made me look stupid, like somebody else, someone I didn't recognize. I tried to shield myself from myself and my surroundings. Not from him, though. I couldn't. The man had steel-trap eyes.

"Control? It seems this hasn't been working. It's like everything that comes out of my mouth is so abstract it can't possibly have come from me, I hardly recognize it."

"We've only just started. Be patient."

"We've only just started this time, though. Right, Caetano? How many times have I been here, how many will I come back?"

"As many as you need."

"Neither of us will ever know."

"Of course not, but we'll keep on trying. Isn't that what life is? A series of trials?"

"Sure. But even so, I don't think this is going to work this time around."

He sat in silence for a moment—I think he was trying to make sure I'd said what he thought I had—then smiled and asked: "Does that worry you?"

"What does?"

"That this won't work."

"Of course."

"And what could go wrong this time?"

"My whole life. I haven't got a house, or friends, I have nothing, Luiza's gone, 'cause she's a vapid *puta*. She's got no humanity, she left me, just like that. How could she? What did I do wrong this time? Nothing, I didn't do anything wrong this time! Was it because of that fucking album? Because I didn't come home earlier? It can't have been."

Something opened up inside me and words started spilling out in a pompous, contiguous jumble. Memories, facts, and lies all fell out of my mouth.

"I can't articulate my thought."

"What do you mean, your thought?"

"It's chaos."

"Chaos?"

"No. My language. It's chaotic, it comes from inside me, from a part of me that's still wild. A part I don't understand. I can't grasp what I'm feeling. If I saw her right this moment, I'm not sure whether I'd kiss her or kill her or, ugh. Things get lost between my head and my mouth—somewhere unknown to me—and they never come back. I'm stuck. I can't reach those things anymore, you know? Not even just to feel them. All that's left here is this senseless knot and it scares me. 'Cause there are times when I'm so good at hiding the truth I don't even recognize the story anymore, and it'd be totally weird if things actually happened the way I said they did. Like fiction. I'm not sure if it's talking or desire that I'm afraid of. Are you following me?"

"You think there's a part of you that's still unknown? Just one? We're all completely unknown to ourselves. That's what this work is all about."

"Yeah . . . in a way. 'Cause, I don't know, it's like I'm stupid. Not in my head, but whenever I open my mouth, the same nagging tone always comes out. And things don't evolve. There I am, trying to break through, and I only manage to scratch the surface. How many times have I been here, exactly? I don't learn. I don't remember things, I can't draw connections, and most of the time, I don't even understand what I've said myself."

"Maybe you're using the wrong part of your body."

"Huh?"

"You try to rationalize everything, analyze everything, scrutinize everything. Try feeling instead. Think about it, about your impulses. Our time's up."

"I hate it when time ends, generally speaking. How much do I owe you?"

"Nothing."

"Nothing, as always. But I insist on asking. Who knows if one day you'll want to charge me."

"We have a deal, remember?"

"I remember. Thanks."

"Is this important to you?"

"That depends. If I said yes would you make me pay you or would you make me find somebody cheaper?"

"Either-or."

"In that case, it's not important."

"Agreed. Till next time."

"Yeah."

I closed the door behind me and headed toward the city center. The street that led there was a deep parabola and I enjoyed watching cars vanish, then emerge at the other end, far away, where there was sunlight. I wanted to be able to do that, to immerse myself in some dark corner of my life only to surface at the other, brighter end of it. An end I figured must exist, one where everything was peaceful and the only turbulence was caused by good and sweet things. But those kinds of ridiculous wishes only existed in dumb self-help books, I knew that. In any case, the center was near, and to reach it, all I had to do was go down, then up again. There was no easy way about it. I would've deep dived into my own hell to reach the other, brighter end of my life, the warm center of the person I wanted to be. "So long as it's not death," I said aloud to myself. I did this a lot whenever I needed to interrupt a train of thought. That is, a part of me still does, that unknown part I can't access and that manifests as sentences spoken in the middle of the street—or in the middle of something. On the actual street, I searched for some trivial thing to pull me away from my negative thoughts, but things struggled to get through to me. Going to the supermarket, the post office, or the home-essentials store was just that, walking with measured steps that said *no, no, no* while my head nodded the exact opposite—but it was all just a consequence of my stride. I pictured myself moving backward, toward the therapist's office. Back up the hillside, my leg weighted rearward, my knee and tiptoes tensed, then my heel meeting the rocky ground. And again on the left. I sit in the green armchair and all the words zip back into me. They leave his ears and meet the breeze coming through the window, making the curtains flutter. I swallow. I feel like I'm articulating the words in reverse. They turn from words back into unformed thoughts. My chest itches on the inside, maybe this is what they were before they became jagged thoughts: an itch in my chest. I rewind further, to before our fight, and see Luiza's saliva—droplets of condensation in the air—return to her tongue along with every harsh word. I watch her suck her sorrow back through her teeth. She stands before me, serene.

Déjà vu. Already on the uphill, I spotted a man and woman changing their car tire in the exact spot where, a decade earlier, my friend Michele and I had changed the tire on her burgundy Kadett. We'd been doing all right at the time, I remembered, we'd never changed a tire before but were doing just great. Until a bunch of guys noticed us and started hanging around laughing and interjecting. Funny, none of them actually offered to help, but they hovered like flies, creating a sort of collective hum, mocking our failures. We finally managed, without any of the help they didn't offer. At the time, I would've been offended if they'd tried. I'm not saying their derision doesn't offend me today, of course it does, but I'd accept an offer to help change a tire, seeing as I've never done it on my own, except for that one time I helped Michele. I stood there for a few minutes watching the man sweat as he turned the wheel wrench, his wife holding the spare tire, the jack, his shirt. My mouth fell a little wider and I noticed the couple giving me a strange look. I hated when I reacted that way. It was as if the doors to the outside world shut entirely while many other, inside doors—each a little deeper within me—opened. And even though I knew I was standing on the sidewalk like an idiot, gawking at strangers, I couldn't help myself. It took me a while to snap out of that state. I shook my head, which was when the pleasantry came out: "Hi! I don't know how to change tires." I dropped my eyes and kept walking, coated in shame. It was a while before the warmth in my face passed, but since I loved to walk, it soon mixed with the heat of physical exertion. I didn't like buses or cabs. I always preferred to walk. To walk until my feet ached and my thoughts ran dry. Besides, walking always dropped me into situations like that couple's; walking gave me the time to watch people, houses, streets, trees, bundles of larvae clinging to leaves, cars—the sheer speed of them—their drivers and passengers, even the expressions draped on their faces; walking gave me time to decide where to look, what to pay attention to. I didn't drive, never would. On buses, scenes sped past too quickly and the only form of observation available was to turn your head back until you could no longer follow the object with your eyes, an alternative I'd never liked. I needed to be able to choose what to watch. If I stood still and a car drove past too quickly, at least I wasn't the one giving up—it was simply the way life had presented things to me. I could decide not to look or instead follow it with my eyes until it disappeared around a bend or down a hill. In any case, it was my decision whether I turned my head or not.

I ran into Luiza at the next corner. Which wasn't choice but chance. My eyes fixed on the image of her.

"Hi," she said like she didn't have a choice.

I would've liked to say something.

Caetano had told me once before that I wasn't in control. That I was never in control. We'd been discussing my fear of flying. When I'm scared, I go limp, quiet, and look like someone awaiting certain death. That's me—every time I get on a plane. I speak normally to people, I might even crack a joke, and I never go into a panic. Not once. But my face turns hard, blank, and sad for however long I'm on the plane, which, really, is just a ton of steel full of flammable fuel. I watch every movie and TV show available, but nothing helps. I used to fear being crushed by an electric garage door. Oddly enough, that fear passed the moment a garage door fell on my head and nothing happened. Just a bump. I'd been certain that sooner or later I'd run into Luiza on the street, either here, in Rio, or at the end of the earth. It didn't matter where, I just knew it would happen. But I never thought it'd be so soon. That's how it went, though. The man with steel-trap eyes had told me I wasn't in control, that at most I had the illusion of control, but that nothing, nothing, was under my purview. That day, in Caetano's office, I gripped the arm-chair's armrests and learned to accept life as imminent and fated, and my eyebrows arched so sharply they were never the same again, lending me a look of perpetual awe.

I wish I'd said something. But all I did was grip the house's low wall as Luiza walked past me, as Luiza turned the corner, as Luiza once again vanished from sight. If in that moment the world were to crumble, if a plane or an overhead door were to crash down on my head, there'd be nothing I could do.

FLOR

Her hair spilled over her shoulders, and she was always in a hat
and canvas shoes, which may have been why she reminded me
a bit of Renato Borghetti, that folk singer with the accordion.
Whenever I think of that time and of that place and try to
remember people's faces, or their voices, she's the one I picture
most clearly.

It was 1988, but thinking of it now, it seems like it could've
been much earlier. Opposite my house stood Mr. Kuntz's shop,
with its dirt floor and exposed brick walls. That's where I spent
most afternoons, with Celoí, Mr. Kuntz's daughter. Celoí's
mom had died in childbirth, which made them, Celoí and
Mr. Kuntz, a very serious pair. I liked going there because it
was right in front of my house and because Celoí had Xuxa's
latest album—the one with "Ilariê," "Abecedário," and "Arco-
íris"—and we'd dance to it in front of her dad's store until six
thirty at night, since we knew the transformer on the street

always blew at seven. Seven p.m., without fail. The transformer probably couldn't handle all the people watching telenovelas, taking showers, switching their radios on, using their blenders, and God knows what else, all at the same time, so it'd start crackling and sparking until boom! For a few hours, no one had electricity and it was like we lived in a far-flung Amazonian village. There were no sidewalks and the cobblestones in the street were totally uneven, which cost all us kids plenty of toenails since that's where we learned to play soccer and to bike, and where we would dance to the latest hits. Not bad for a modest neighborhood on the border of Campo Bom and Novo Hamburgo.

Our house sat between two garages: the Klein family's—a dad, a mom, and their little daughter, all blond with alarmingly blue eyes, whose names I can't really remember—and, on the other side, the one run by the most striking figure of my childhood, a woman whose face I saw only a couple of times but never forgot. Both garages had a decent enough clientele, but there was a sort of tension between the two shops that seeped through the walls of our house from both sides.

My parents were friends with the Klein family so we often had lunch together on weekends. My brother and I would play with their daughter, who was my brother's age, I think—it's all a bit of a blur. What's stuck with me most from those gatherings is a phrase I once heard said: How could a *machorra* like that do such a thing? And curious kid that I was, I immediately asked: What's a *machorra*? Total silence. Followed by my mom laughing really weirdly, clearly embarrassed. The men scratched their heads and stared into their beers. The Klein mom was so horrified to hear that word come out of my mouth that she started laughing, too. Mom tried to salvage the situation. *Cachorra*, like a dog, she said, *cachorra*. But I was sure I'd heard *machorra*, so I insisted, but they just changed the subject and ignored me. Except they weren't expecting me to hang off their every word, to prick up my ears until they found their way back to that subject. So I stayed quiet and eavesdropped while feigning interest in a doll, my attention focused entirely on them. That's when I understood that they were talking about our other neighbor. She was the *machorra*.

The next day, I was leaning over the wall, trying to catch a glimpse of her, when I heard the crunching of her canvas shoes getting closer and stretched myself farther over the wall . . . and fell. She ran over to help me and I remember hearing her voice, just like a fairy's, asking if I was all right, if I was hurt. Mom ran out of the house, lifted me by the wrists, and dragged me back to our patio. I heard a thank-you from Mom and a you're-welcome from our neighbor followed by the sound of someone sucking on a *cuia*. I turned to Mom and asked her why our neighbor was a *machorra*. The slurping stopped abruptly. Mom's face turned bright red as she dragged me into the house and asked me where I'd heard that word. Yesterday, at lunch, I said. The canvas shoes crackled over the hard earth as they rushed toward the garage. Mom leaned against the sink, both hands over her face, and sighed in a way that sounded terribly worried. I just stood there, wiping the dirt off my elbows and making sure the rest of me was fine, too; I'd fallen off a wall, after all, and my mom, strangely, seemed totally unconcerned. Honey, you can't say those kinds of things to people. What kind of things and what kind of people was she talking about, I asked—I honestly couldn't remember—and she answered with a pinch on the shoulder. My shoulder wasn't hurt, but my feelings sure were, so I went to my room to cry. Between sobs, I tried to think of what a *machorra* could possibly be, and why it had offended our neighbor and upset mom so much. I made up my mind to ask again. It's a sickness, honey. The neighbor's sick. I went back to my room, nearly satisfied with her response. If it was a sickness, why hadn't they just said so? I kept wondering whether it was contagious but decided it couldn't be. The garage was always busy, after all. I went back to the kitchen. Mom, what kind of sickness? My mom raised her hand to her face again and took a deep breath. It's from the rusty metal they keep in the junkyard. I didn't know you could get sick from metal, but I felt satisfied with her response when, the next day, our teacher explained tetanus to the class.

The following morning, I did what anyone would do for a neighbor who's sick, or at least what I thought, in my kid brain, anyone would do: I took her flowers. I'd seen it on TV. I picked some of the flowers that grew around my house, real wildflowers, a couple of yellow ones and a bunch of daisies, then walked over to the mechanic's—real early so no one would see me—and left the flowers at her door, in a glass of water. I also left a little note wishing she'd get well soon and asking her to please put the flowers in a vase and return the glass because my mom would probably notice it was missing. At noon, on my way home, I saw that the flowers were gone and smiled, happy she'd taken them. I walked into my house feeling cheerful, with a spring in my step, but as soon as I saw my mom's face and the glass that had held the flowers in her hand, and heard her voice asking what had gotten into me, my mood was shattered. I explained to her that if the neighbor really had a case of *machorra*, whatever it was, someone had to go over there and wish her a speedy recovery. Which is what I did. My mom gave me a big hug and said I was such a good girl, which was why I shouldn't play near the garage anymore. I asked which one and she said the neighbor's. Then I asked her if I could still go play at Mr. Klein's. Yes, she said, so I went out to see Celoí—I didn't want to play in either shop anyway.

Celoí put Xuxa on and we danced between bags of beans and stacks of red floor wax. I remembered then that my mom was always buying that wax but our floor wasn't red and I didn't quite understand why, but just as I was about to ask Celoí about the wax, the neighbor walked in. I stopped dancing and stood there, petrified. My first thought was that when a person's sick they should stay in bed, so I asked her: Are you feeling better, ma'am? She turned to me, her wet hair over her face, and with pink, pink lips and kind, honey-colored eyes, she said she'd never been better. She thanked me for the flowers and kneeled to give me a kiss. Just then, my mom showed up and dragged me out by the hair. As we left, I heard Celoí's dad saying, Don't worry about it, Flor.

Flor, her name was Flor. And she really looked like a flower, too. Actually, her whole name was Florlinda, "lovely flower." I asked Celoí about it the next day and told her about the sickness. Celoí rolled her eyes the way people do when they're accusing someone of being naive, said nothing, took me by the hand and into her room, then grabbed a teddy bear and two Barbies. Okay, so they weren't real Barbies, they were knockoffs, but they were affordable and they worked just fine for what she was trying to explain. I was eight years old and Celoí was eleven or twelve. She took one of the dolls and the teddy bear and began her explanation. This is a man and this is a woman. When they both love each other, they go into their bedroom and then they go like this—she put one toy on top of the other—your mom and dad do this and that's why you exist, and why your brother does, too. I nodded, trying to follow her demonstration. Then she took the two dolls and did the same thing and said: Some people do this instead. That's *machorra*, but my dad said it isn't nice to say that.

Mr. Kuntz was a quiet man, but he knew how to take care of people. He and Flor were friends. I'd often seen them sipping *chimarrão* together in her backyard or in front of his shop. I thought they were in love, so I asked Celoí about it. She slapped me and, annoyed, asked if I hadn't understood what she'd just explained to me with the dolls. But the fact was a doll's a doll, a bear's a bear, and a *machorra*'s a *machorra*. Celoí tried again: Okay, let's see, what do you like more, dolls or cars? Well, it depends on the car and on the doll. Celoí rolled her eyes like she had before. What do you like more, dancing to Xuxa or playing tag? I didn't know how to answer that, either, because everything depended, really, and I was having trouble understanding what she was getting at. Okay, do you like the color pink or the color blue? I like green. For God's sake, this is your last chance. Who do you like more, me or Claudinho? Claudinho was a boy who lived on our street; Celoí thought he was cute. You, of course, I said. Then you're a *machorra*, she said, impatient.

I went home that day with my head hanging low and, as I crossed the street, ran right into Flor, who was standing between our gate and the electricity meter. Why the long face, sweetie? Because Celoí thinks I'm sick, too, that I've got what you have. I dragged my sneakers along the gravel. She bent over and put her hand on my forehead, as if I had the flu and she was trying to take my temperature. Don't be silly, there's nothing wrong with you. You're doing just great. I looked up at her to see if she looked like she was telling me the truth. She brushed her hair away from her face, and just then, the transformer blew. The sparks lit up her eyes, and in that moment, she was the prettiest flower I'd ever seen.

BOOTS

She trailed her boots through the mud. It was the only way she could move forward, outward. She's dead, she thought. Dead. Despite what I said, all I begged, how many promises I made, how many nights I lost, how young we are. Were. Are. I still am. Nothing, none of it mattered. She's dead, she thought, eyes fixed on the muddy red puddle where her reflection contorted. One of those things you don't believe can happen. The elevator plummeted, they were hit by a bus, they fell and cracked their neck, they got terminal cancer, choked on an olive pit, slipped on the sidewalk and banged their head, drowned, got in a car accident, were hit by a stray bullet. It was none of that. Suicide. She'd taken some of the junk she had at home, gulped it down. She wondered how it'd happened.

This is how. K arrived home in that thick sadness that had enveloped her for months. She sat on the sofa and for a few seconds waited to see whether she felt anything. She'd made up her mind. It was nothing, they said, nothing, chin up. But it was a disjoining, a sense of unbelonging, of having been torn from the world, beaten far from what we understand love to be. It wasn't pretty. No, feeling that way was cold, ugly, painful, lonely. No one could take her away from that place. Not even Fran. She opened a bottle of vodka and had one glass, then another, and another. Only then did she reach for the pills. A pack of Frontal, Rivotril, Anafranil, a pack of Lexotan, of Tylenol. She popped all the remaining blisters, opened every capsule. For a moment, she wondered why she had so much medication. She dropped them one by one into the empty glass as she smoked a cigarette. She raked her hand over her head a few times, enjoying the prickliness of her hair as it grew out. With her finger, she drew the contour of the scar above her ear, almost at the back of her head. She got up off the living room sofa and went to the kitchen for a spoon. She wasn't crying. The worst agony of all was the one that stopped her from feeling. She started crushing the pills. She added a splash of vodka, then mixed it into a paste. White particles danced as she moved the spoon through the liquid. She got up again, set her electric razor to two, and shaved all her hair off without looking. She ran her hands over her head again and felt good. She filled the glass halfway with vodka, filled her eyes to the brim. A whitish mixture. She drank it in three gulps and finished smoking her cigarette. She fell into a pleasant lethargy. Her head was light, as if in a trance. There were sporadic shocks in her body, as if someone was swinging at her from inside.

They only found K Wednesday night. They broke into her apartment after Fran insisted something was wrong. They found her with her head in her hands, like she was trying to protect herself from something.

Twenty-four hours after finding the body, Fran was still in the living room, picturing the scene on repeat. She wasn't trying to make sense of it anymore, she was just curious. No. She felt the need to participate in it. She got up and slipped on K's brown boots, which had been too tight on K, but that didn't matter anymore.

Fran didn't attend the wake, she didn't want to hold that last, static image.

On one of those afternoons when they talked about everything, K had told her she wanted to be cremated. She spoke of the body evaporating when incinerated. Twelve hundred degrees Celsius, and seconds later, you're just dust and mineral remains. Fran wasn't listening. She pretended to but instead sang cheerful songs in her head. She knew that if she paid attention, that image would etch itself inside her, another useless fear, another worry to lug about with her.

"When I die, I want to be cremated. I've already put it in writing."

"Does it cost a lot?"

"Not the burning part, what's expensive is being kept in the fridge beforehand."

"The fridge?"

"Never mind."

They laughed.

"I had a weird dream."

"Tell me."

"A building was on fire, and instead of leaving, I went back for my computer. I watched my skin burn and boils blossom and then burst, one after another. My skin was flayed off, leaving me exposed, so exposed that if a cool breeze had whipped past I would've been ripped to shreds. When I got out, I saw a lake and wanted immediately to dive into it. But I knew the water wouldn't soothe the pain. Instead, each droplet would seep into my wounds, making them heavy, waterlogged, even more painful. Making it harder for them to heal. That's when I woke up."

"What a horrifying dream."

"And you know what, Fran? That's how I feel. Completely disfigured. Covered in bulky, disgusting sores that never heal. That will always cause disgust. Inside me. Neither hugs nor caresses nor anything else is comforting, because I feel so disgusted. When someone touches me, I feel scared, repulsed. Like I might dirty that person with my pus, like they're going to infect my wounds. Any mention of intimacy fills me with dread." And she paused. "It's different with you. I don't know why, but it's like, with you, things are better."

"They are. I can tell."

Silence.

Fran had heard stories of K killing a classmate in college. She'd been trying to defend herself against a group of three. K had never told her about it, though, she'd never mentioned the subject. Because K didn't talk about it, Fran never knew whether it had happened. But she knew it'd been awful. The family had left the state, K had dropped out of college, and she'd ended up there, near Fran. She can't even say exactly how they met, maybe through the friend of a friend of a friend, or on the street. They'd seen each other and immediately understood one another. The sort of thing that's so rare you don't question it. K's journey was a mystery. Fran didn't know where she'd been, didn't know what path she'd taken or the dark roads she'd walked till then. All she knew was that they'd had to come up with new words for their feelings—the words they had weren't enough, at least not enough for K. And Fran tried.

"Why did you come back for the computer?"

"Huh?"

"In the dream."

"It doesn't matter."

"Why not?"

"I've spent a long time wondering why I went back for that computer. But it could have been anything, you know, anyone.

Why do I keep searching for things in hell? I'm trying. I want to try. It's me, you see? I'm not well. I'm on my way. Thinking of why. I'll be all right. Thinking about stuff helps me get to important places."

"And have you reached any conclusions?"

"I still don't understand most of the reasons or the places, but at least I'm visiting them. I dunno."

"Whatever happened, it wasn't your fault, K."

Then K killed herself, and Fran stood at the door to the crematorium thinking of everything she'd said on the afternoon they'd talked about anything and everything, thinking of K's flayed body, of boil after boil, all in a matter of seconds. The scent of burnt flesh. A photograph that glows red, forms a hole, and is then consumed completely. Bitter heat in memories that turn to dust and evaporate in a hot gust of wind. It was for the best that they evaporated, she thought. Memories are easier to hold on to in that light, gaseous state. A burst of heat and a reddish picture, impossible to discern. Memory and nothing else. She couldn't do anything. Suddenly, she was at the door to the crematorium, staring fixedly at a blind spot. A spot that made Fran burn alongside her, because there was nothing she could do—she didn't know how.

Her feet were bound by K's tight boots and by the urge to retrace her steps. She wanted to do everything in her power to seek out the hint of an answer, a sign, a symptom, but she just didn't understand. She trailed her boots through the mud.

Light rain sprayed down on her, soaking through her woolen jacket, weighing down her body. The weight pressed into the soles of the boots, which, in turn, sank into the cemetery mud. No answers came to Fran.

Later, she dreams of K. She dreams they are chatting, gazing out at the night through the large living room window, and as Fran looks away for a moment, K jumps. Fran watches her fall. She doesn't look down, at the sidewalk, but instead up, straight north, and waits for K to reappear.

MY COUSIN'S IN TOWN

I opened the apartment door, saw the bathroom light, and heard the water running in the shower: cue panic. My work colleagues looked at me, and I looked back at them, paralyzed. Thinking back on it now, it seems funny, but at the time it was awful. I just wanted to host dinner at home. You do certain things to fit in when you've got a new apartment and a new job. I'd decided to take advantage of the fact that Bruna was traveling to invite my work colleagues over. Only I hadn't told any of them about Bruna. It just wasn't done where I worked. Bruna's a designer. I can't say for sure, but maybe these sorts of things are easier to accept in her world. I go out for dinner with Bruna's friends, her work friends. They know we're a couple because Bruna doesn't have any hang-ups about it. I do. I mean, I've had more in the past, but I'm handling the whole sexuality thing better now—in my head, of course. I don't tell a lot of people about it. Some don't need to know, it doesn't make a difference. My work colleagues, for example, don't need to know, neither does my family. My family loves Bruna, they just think it's weird that she lives with me. After all, she's a grown woman with a fairly stable career. They think that by now she should be married and living with her amazing husband. Except then they contradict themselves: Ah, well, that's how things are these days, people marry later, first they've got to go to school, to build up their little nest egg, and only then do they think of starting a family, Bruna's got it right. The thing is, Bruna and I *are* family. It just took me a while to realize. It happened one day when I was seriously ill and considering spending the night at my parents'. Bruna got really ticked off, and rightly so. That was our house, I could feel comfortable and safe there—that's how I started getting the picture. With the smell of soap and bread, and with stupid decisions we had to make like what color the furniture should be and whether to hang curtains. That's how I started to get what family meant, with dishes piling up and hairs scattered across the floor, hairs that were long and black because both Bruna and I have long black hair. My family was right there in the dishes and the flu, in the hair and the smell of a home-cooked meal, in breakfast in bed and hot showers, in quarrels and apologies, in affection, love, and care. And we really were a family, even as we watched TV or walked our imaginary dog in the park on Sunday afternoons. It's not that we didn't like pets, we just didn't want one at that moment, neither of us had the time or disposition for a pet. Instead we had a running joke about being the cool lesbian couple who walks their dog on Sunday afternoons. We took Frida, our dog with a Mexican temper, for walks in the park and laughed whenever we threw her imaginary ball and laughed even harder whenever we gave her an imaginary treat and didn't scoop the imaginary turd she'd just done in the seedbed of the house across the street. It's all very low key, though, and we've got these jokes we can't share with other people, because they're more weird than they are funny, but it's the weird stuff that brings people closer together. I love Bruna and I've never wanted to hurt her and never will want to hurt her. We have this deal where we don't say things we might regret later and never, ever threaten to end the relationship unless it's a real possibility, or rather, unless it's something the person actually, legitimately wants for the future. Things were even better after we reached this agreement. We've had this sort of complicity, which keeps us safe from having to share our horrendous jokes with other people, and safe from having to face up to the fact that though we might read books and visit exhibitions—which is sort of de rigueur in our artsy, pseudocult, pseudointellectual lesbian milieu—we also watch TV shows like *Faustão*, *Big Brother*, telenovelas, and *Honey Boo Boo* (all dubbed, by the way), and, finally, safe from being unloved. Because we both have each other's backs, we have each other covered, and we love one another in that simple way. And only I know how annoying Bruna can be when she's ill and how anxious she gets right before handing in a project; only I know that her anxiety makes her face break out and her heart race at night, robbing us both of sleep, because I worry, too, and though I might tell her a hundred times over that she'll do just fine, only I know she won't believe me; only me. And only she knows how annoying I can be about totally pointless stuff like not getting the dry dish towel dirty or sitting on the sofa cushions; only she knows how annoying I can be about how I think clothes should be folded and books arranged on the shelves and in the bathroom; only she knows, even though this is what every couple the world over is like; when it comes to the two of us, only we know. And what matters is believing we're the only ones. But life's never good or easy enough that things are perfect; sometimes, we don't understand each other, and sometimes, she says things that offend me, and even though she says she didn't say them on purpose or that that's not what she meant, I still feel hurt and offended, and she knows that what I need then is silence, while I know that what she needs is to talk, and we keep trying to find ways to make our life work together. I'll bite my lip and try to sleep, though I can see how anxious she is—she really didn't want to upset me—and she'll come over and give me a hug and try to talk to me, even though I can't and she knows I can't, and that's when we get each other, because we know one another. And it's hard for the same reasons when I'm the one who does or doesn't do something and she's the one who gets upset: she wants to talk and

I can't, but we each try, all relative to our sense of urgency and hurt. Up to now, things have been good, even after I walked in the door with three workmates who had no clue who Bruna was and even after she came out of the bathroom wrapped in a towel and said hello, and I introduced her to everyone; even so, things are still working out. I'm throwing a dinner at home, I told Bruna then, and she looked at me suspiciously, already aware of what was going on. So she said she'd come back early from her trip because the trade show had been boring and she'd felt like it. And my colleagues stood there all the while, not quite knowing what was going on, while Bruna waited for me to say something, for me to explain who these people were.

Bruna, these are my work colleagues.

Girls, this is Bruna. My cousin. She's in town for an exam. The ENEM.

Bruna looked at my colleagues and said hello to them as if the whole cousin thing and the whole ENEM thing were the most ordinary truths in the world. Then she excused herself to go study. I stayed in the kitchen with the girls and the food tore its way down my throat all night long. After they left, I went to talk to Bruna and all she said was that at some point things would have to change. Then she laughed at the ridiculousness of it all and said the truth would've been painless, but . . . maybe, she wasn't sure, maybe she was wrong. The fact is, we're still trying.

DREAMING

The bottle spun and spun, and with each rotation I thought:
Please, fuck, let it not be me. Said and done. It was my turn.
The bottle ogled me with its orifice. Rochelle and the little
games she cooked up to make people uncomfortable, like we
were still teenagers. Whatever, I just had to answer a couple of
crummy questions. Because people have questions. I knew that
things were different with me. I was withdrawn, so everybody
thought I had no stories to tell, that I'd experienced absolutely
nothing. *What should we ask reserved, cagey Raquel?* They rolled
their eyes trying to think of something inoffensive to ask. I've
got to say, I was kind of sick of that ridiculous game. So I
downed my glass of wine, swiped Tassi's glass, drank hers, then
swiped Elisa's. There. Everybody gave me a concerned look.
Right, awesome. Girls, I'm going to tell you about something
that happened while I was living in the United States. I think
only Rochelle knew me back then. What's up, Rach, you gonna

tell us about that time you dyed your hair auburn? They all laughed. Well, yeah, there was that. But there was also Mel. They looked at each other and then at me like I was the biggest weirdo on the planet. I find your lack of imagination kind of tiresome. Okay, let's put it like this. You look at me and you see Raquel, a responsible businesswoman who never cheats on her taxes and always does everything just right. You look at me and you think: a woman like Raquel, who's so shockingly tedious, has probably never tested her boundaries. Well, I wanted to test my boundaries, so I did. I'll start the story where it matters, when I moved to a place near Castro. Do I need to explain what Castro is? Silence. Oh God, please just watch *Milk* already, 'kay? That'll make things clearer. And, of course, make the appropriate temporal leap.

I couldn't help laughing when I saw their faces. Part out of nervousness, part out of embarrassment, part out of a sense of vindication. Tassi looked skeptical but engaged. Elisa seemed kind of scared, and Rochelle was curious and smug.

I'm sure I told you about this. Didn't I, Rô? Never! I haven't got a clue what this whole Mel thing is about. Well, then I'll start with the day I met Mel, at the house party of a person I never laid eyes on. It was BYOB, and I brought a bottle of whisky. Mel brought the same, which is what got us talking. We saw our respective bottles, and she walked up to me and asked whether I liked it—seeing as it was cheap and all—and I said yes. I laughed and said it was decent enough booze. We sat on a low wall behind the house, smoking, drinking, and chatting. She was from California. Blonde, leggy, tanned. She had a surfer's face, cheeks permanently sunburnt. A cliché. A friend of hers asked if we wanted some coke and I said yes because Mel had said yes like it was nothing. We handed over the money. I was honestly convinced the guy was just going to run off with his fistful of dollars, but no, a half hour later, we each had our little baggies of cocaine. We took our first two lines right there on the wall over a pocket mirror. Coke's sort of hard to pin down, don't you think? You become super outgoing, I mean, expansive; I remember gesturing a lot. Don't you think coke can have that effect?

They were all silent. Oh, I see, you've never done any. But Tassi shook her head and said she had, once. I told her it didn't count. You're only allowed to have an opinion on coke if you really lose control, like actually. I think any worthwhile experience with drugs has to include a loss of control. And if it doesn't, just shut up and go get high again, 'cause clearly you did something wrong.

Our bottle was half-empty by the time the cops came through. It was intense, but Mel told me to relax. She said cops can't go barging into houses, that we might just have to go back inside and turn the volume down for a few minutes or for as long as it took the cop cars and sirens to be out of earshot. Everything'd go back to normal then. Worst-case scenario, we'd just have to go home, she said. And the idea of going home sort of moved something inside me. Maybe it was exhaustion, or maybe that's when I realized what I'd been doing.

Mel's friends came back with more coke and an invite to break into a mansion that was empty that weekend and swim in their pool. Mel didn't flinch, she just said, Finally, someone's found a house with a pool. There were eight of us, I think. The other thirty-odd people kept on drinking. As I walked through the living room, I saw a guy passed out beside a puddle of puke and two girls making out in an armchair; a black woman sat topless with her legs spread wide while an underage-looking blonde sat in her lap. One's hand was in the other's pants, and apparently, things were going so well neither of them cared what was going on around them. I lingered, watching them, then felt Mel grab my fist with her hand and lead me to the exit.

My bottle was empty by the time we reached the mansion, and I realized I'd been swept along by some sort of Bling Ring. The house belonged to some celebrity. I can't remember who, just that it was someone famous.

The girls interrupted me to ask how come I didn't know who the owners were. After all, it was the most important bit of information from that evening. I reminded them that I'd already had a bottle of whisky and a whole baggie of cocaine. Between sips of the questionable chardonnay Rochelle had brought with her, they went quiet.

So we jumped the fence, which was ridiculous—just some bushes held up by wire—and everybody started stripping to get in the water. I looked over at Mel, who was pulling her shirt off over her head, undoing her belt, and rolling her pants down to her knees, stomping everything off until she was naked. A cluster of necklaces sat between her small, rosy breasts. I was kind of stunned—she was gorgeous. I couldn't fully grasp her beauty. You know when that happens? When someone's so beautiful you feel kind of skeptical about it, and you can't quite get your head around it? Well, that's what it was like. Before heading to the pool, she walked over to me, brandished the bottle, and asked if I wanted another sip. I took a swig and stripped, holding her gaze. She tugged me by the arm. Seconds later I was blowing bubbles through my nose. Both water and night were warm. I surfaced from the dive and felt hands around my waist and my mouth covered by Mel's chapped lips. I kept my eyes closed as I kissed and tried to get air. I think that may have confused things a little. I got out of the pool and sat on a chaise longue. Mel came after me, asking what had happened, if she'd done anything wrong. I said no and kissed her on the cheek. She said, Got it, and that was it. I looked around me and thought: I'm twenty years old and one day I'll be sitting at a table telling a shocking story to a group of boring friends. This had to be it. Mel started getting up and I grabbed her by the arm, asked if there was more whisky, more coke, and she said there was always more. We kissed again. I kept on trying to get air, this time because I needed it. She asked me if I wanted to go home with her, I suggested my place. She agreed.

It was lovely to walk those steep streets at dawn. We felt absurdly safe. In the US, everything unfolds as if onstage. Curtains open onto moons that glimmer in the ocean over the rooftops of colonial houses, wood gables, white fences, and porches with swings that sit invitingly empty. What's more, San Francisco felt atemporal, like you might run into Patti Smith and Robert Mapplethorpe in the 1960s—on a fugitive cross-country trip, in tight pants, necklaces, open shirts—or like you'd turn a corner in Castro and find yourself marching alongside Harvey Milk. I don't know if I felt like this on account of my inspirations or what. In any case, I didn't believe in the 2000s. Not there. There were other, more plausible scenarios. I've always had a nostalgic streak, always wanted to live in another decade. Seeing Mel standing at the gate to my house with her disheveled, hippieish hair made that scene seem real.

I stopped and looked at the hill we'd just walked up, and Mel asked if that was where I lived. I said yes, but that I had roommates, so we had to be quiet. Drunk people are always sort of out of touch, aren't they? We walked up the stairs and I closed the door to my room. Urgency undressed us and swallowed up the night. I'm not sure if we made much noise, I can't remember. The truth was, I'd never wanted to go home with Mel. The next day, still in bed, she told me she wanted to see Rio. I said I lived in Rio, except in the south, in a city called Porto Alegre, and she said she'd never heard of it. I wasn't surprised. She asked me what the name meant, so I translated it for her: Joyful Harbor, I waxed poetic. She thought it was funny. Over the next few days, she called, went looking for me at work, and showed up at my house at inappropriate hours. I did what I could to shut down her advances, but she wouldn't give up. She said I should open myself up to the good things in life. I told her I had. And that I'd had enough. Right then, all I wanted was to leave. I left Mel a letter. She kept writing me emails. I never answered them. Eventually, she gave up. We never spoke again.

The girls were still quietly sipping from the same glasses of wine. No one asked questions or challenged the truth of what I said. Because none of them believed my story. Not even I was totally sure things had happened the way I said they had. I think it's mostly true, though. No matter. I was Raquel, the chaste one, and that was what shocked them.

RENFIELD'S DEMONS

Red curtains. Dust. Leonard Cohen records. Shoes. Walls that rise to a vaulted ceiling. Numbed wrists. Débora has been tied up for four hours. Someplace strange. There are two purplish bruises around her wrists. She lifts her head and, for a few seconds, gazes at moths on the curtains and at a kind of small altar embedded in a black wall. Words. Wax-pastel drawings. Candles. Books with gold lettering on the spines. Statues. She can't place them. Débora is suspended from a thick sisal rope whose raw-leather ends hang from two hooks attached to the wall. She wouldn't be in this situation if she could stand, but her legs are limp. Her knees are bent partway and her head rests on her left arm. Vanessa returns to the room with a glass of water. She wears long fake eyelashes. Long fake eyelashes and nothing else. She approaches Débora. Eyelashes tickle her back. Water, Vanessa whispers. Débora closes her eyes and moves her head up and down. Vanessa presses her body into Débora's back and touches the glass to her mouth. Débora immediately drinks. Easy now. Vanessa touches her mouth to the back of Débora's neck. And moves down. A welt swells around her neck. Droplets of blood form languorously over Débora's skin. Vanessa spills the remaining water on this stain. She runs her tongue over all the now-dissolved red microdots. She slurps and feels a primal pleasure. Débora turns around. She wraps her legs around Vanessa's waist. The pressure on her wrists eases. For a second, her eyes clear. She glimpses a statue and doesn't recognize it. The night thunders. Débora loses focus, air, all the strength she has left. They bite one another, kiss, pant.

A week earlier, Débora comes home early. She has a migraine and can barely open her eyes. All she sees are tiny demons capering on her left shoulder. Hooved demons stomping in circles, as the migraine fills her head completely and tenses her neck. A vein bulges. Or an artery. She can't say. She heard it's arteries, not veins, that pulse. Only when blood is clean and new—racing to carry oxygen to every cell—do things pulse. Débora doesn't buy it. Veins pulse at her temple, even when rife with old, asphyxiated blood. Débora turns the key to the door and through half-closed eyes—as if it were possible to curb the pain or at the very least stop the demons from boring through her eye sockets—sees Moira lying on the living room floor. A head with hair that fans out, cascades, and blends in with the rug lies on Moira's belly. It belongs to a woman with a bony back who, on seeing Débora, is shocked. Moira stays on the living room floor, naked, speechless. Her arms are out-stretched, and she bites her lower lip in discomfort. She closes her eyes as if in doing so she, too, could become invisible. The demons stomp on Débora's head, stomp on her breasts, and tunnel into her chest. They plunge into an artery and, flowing against the bloodstream, find the path to her heart, where they carry on their dance of devastation. Débora continues down the hallway to the bathroom, opens the cabinet, grabs their home-pharmacy box, and takes out two pills for her bitch of a headache. She says *bitch of a headache* out loud. She closes the cabinet, leaves the bathroom, goes back in, takes two sleeping pills, and decides to lie down. Before falling asleep, she thinks about how it's just the aftermath. The aftermath of a quarrel. A quarrel that's been looming for months. Months that were cruel. Cruel as the image of Moira and that woman in her living room. She sleeps.

Débora wakes up the next day. It's two in the afternoon on a lazy Friday. No one's home. Only Débora and her demons, all of them quiet. Once she moves, they will stir, kick-starting the pain in her head and heart. But there's nothing she can do about it. It's the demons again. Débora gets up. She lugs herself to the kitchen. What is this bullshit? She can't figure out what's going on—the sun's singeing her eyes and the pills aren't working, at least not anymore. She feels like she's float-ing, cold. She grabs a bottle from the fridge. Wine, she thinks. She pulls the curtains shut. She sits on the sofa and stares at the floor, at the spot where Moira fucked that skank. She says *that skank* out loud. She looks past a stain in the rug. She pulls the stopper out with her teeth and spits it out along with cork bits. Expensive wine, cork stopper. She drinks. It's off. Off. Distance. *Saudade. Saudade.* Moira. She often does this word association exercise, recommended to her by a holistic, mind-free-talking therapist. Five connections are enough to locate the problem. It's a startlingly easy way to create focus. The mind works for you. She drinks the rest of the wine. Goes to the bathroom, opens the mirror cabinet, pulls out the home-pharmacy box, takes two more sleeping pills. She goes back to bed. Gets up, goes back, takes another.

It's night, and Débora has no idea what day it is. Her cell phone's dead. She recalls a strange dream in which Moira tried to wake her up, then apologized and slammed the door shut behind her, in tears. She opens her eyes. Looks for the charger and switches on her cell phone. Fucking *puta*. She opens her eyes again. Three hours. She opens her eyes again. Six hours. She gets up and goes to the bathroom. She opens the mirror cabinet, takes out the little box, knocks back two more.

Uninterrupted sirens. Débora's head trembles as if resting on the window of a moving bus. And stops. It trembles again. And stops. The sirens are unceasing. Débora looks up at the headboard and notes that her cell phone is ringing. She yanks the plug so she can switch it off. The siren continues. She realizes now that the sound isn't a siren, it's Björk's "Pluto." The worst ringtone of all time, Moira used to say. Débora knew something was off the moment they moved in together. She looks at the text message, missed call, and email icons. There are too many to get her head around. Inside, silence. Outside, the sound of traffic and construction. The day starts taking shape in Débora's head. She drops the cell phone. Gets up. Goes to the bathroom, opens the cabinet, grabs the box, the packet is empty. She takes off her shirt, her pants, her panties are dirty with blood. So that's the source of the headache. She turns on the shower, lets the water run. For hours. At times, the water falls crystalline, at others pinkish. She pees. She can feel the heat of her own piss streaming down her thighs, knees, and ankles, then mixing with the water and suds around the drain, tinging the white tile a golden hue. She turns the shower off, walks to her bedroom, and falls into the bed. Dust flits in a ray of sunshine that quickly vanishes.

Knights and dragons take their positions on a mountain. The mouth of one of the creatures opens and flames come licking toward her. The sword falls. Her head rolls. She wakes up.

Débora is sitting at the kitchen counter. Her stomach aches and she feels dizzy. She eats a slice of cake and drinks some tea. Moira has left and there's no trace of her in the apartment. No clothes, no books, none of her crap. They never had any photos. Idiot. Cake. Yeast. Yeast. Air. This time, she is faster, her logic sharper, the urgency more acute. She slams the door and leaves. Her holistic, mind-free-talking therapist would be proud.

So that's it, she thinks as she treads carefully over the flowers freshly planted in the dark earth in front of the building next door. Moira has finally been caught, she's finally left. Débora feels like crying but can't. The demons have guzzled all her tears. Nearly all of her feelings. She knew from the beginning that Moira was a mistake. But she couldn't extricate herself from their codependence. It wasn't their first betrayal, they'd both tried to find in others what they'd lacked from each other. But in their own house, on the living room floor, that was an act of violence: an attempt to find a rock that'd hurt when hurtled at her face. And it was—hurtled. She closes her eyes as the pain from the rock's blow pierces her skull. She's hungry. She goes to the supermarket, buys bread, chocolate, a bottle. A bottle of whatever, the first thing her hand reaches for in the liquor section. She pays. Walks out. Keeps walking. She sits on the wall of the neighboring building with the bag dangling between her legs and kicks a heartsease flower back into the seedbed. A piece of paper tumbles under her feet. *Costume party. Friday 13th @ 11 p.m.* What day is it today? Thursday, answers the doorman, looking accusatory. He probably saw Débora trampling the flowers.

The windows are closed and Débora is on the sofa. She spots a brown stain on the rug. She turns on the TV and sits there, stupefied, for hours. She opens the packet of bread.

Eats a slice. Opens the chocolate. Opens the bottle, drinks, spits, drinks, swallows. She chews more bread. Spits. Drops the already-half-empty bottle on the floor. She closes her eyes. Then opens them. She shuts her hand over shards of glass, then squeezes. Releases.

It's night. The blood on Débora's hands is dry. Friday the thirteenth, eleven p.m. She washes her hands and walks out. She walks down the street along the park, past trees. It's dark. Débora feels no fear, she feels nothing. She comes across a group of grotesque people standing in line and knows she has arrived. Glow-in-the-dark skeletons, monsters, pale odalisques, witches, morbid ballerinas, demons, people in drag. She walks up the steps. Buys a drink. The spasmodic light makes Débora crave one of those pills; it'd be paradise, she thinks. Shredded superheroes, mummies, dismembered zombies, people in masks. Débora moves. No, Débora dances. The music is a brutal pile-drive drone, still she shakes her head and shoulders as if she could exorcise the layers of lethargy enveloping her. And the demons. She cries, a parched silence. A vampire. A vampire looks inside her. She presses a glass to Débora's lips. Débora drinks. The vampire presses her forehead to Débora's and bares her pointed teeth. She fingers her hair. Her mouth descends toward her neck and takes a hard bite. Débora is afraid. It's the first time she's felt anything in days. She closes her eyes and carries on dancing. She drinks. Forgets. Grows weak. Her mouth is wet with the woman's saliva and she feels a peculiar drowsiness that comes and goes with the lights. She grows soft. She follows. Her legs slacken but she can walk. She dies, wakes up. Dies again.

She dances to a slow tune. Raises one arm, the other wrapped around the body of a tall woman with black hair that cascades down her bony back. An organ sounds. Débora rubs her face in the woman's belly, as if trying to wake from a dream in which her head is rolling down a flight of stairs. The woman holds Débora's arms and ties her hands together in a bow with leather strips that she then fastens to hooks on the ceiling. The woman dominates, extenuates, debilitates. She runs her tongue between her legs. Stops just before the scream. That woman is Vanessa, the same one who days earlier was in her living room. With her tongue between Moira's legs. But Débora doesn't know this. She'll never know this.

Débora is tied up. Vanessa finds her artery. It pulses arrhythmically. Débora rehearses a scream. Falls quiet. Vanessa bites, sucks, swallows, bites, sucks, and spits the demons out.

HERMETIC DRAMATURGE

To: talk2anubispipi@gmail.com

nausea

Hey,

I can't sleep. Haven't been able to for days. I don't know, I was thinking about life and suddenly I felt like talking to you. I know it's been a while since we've seen each other. You don't have to answer this email, I just really felt like I was having this conversation with you. Do you know that feeling? That certain topics can only be discussed with certain people? In any case, I don't know if it's because of this "job"—I'm teaching, not sure if you're aware, and since you're a teacher, too, I thought maybe, you know. Anyway, I'll start from the beginning.

The last time we saw each other was 2007, before I went to live in Chile. From Chile, I traveled to Mexico, then crossed the Atlantic and hit Portugal, Spain, England, France, and the Netherlands. I returned to Brazil in 2010, I think. But I didn't stay long. Soon I was on a flight to Asia. I visited Bangladesh, Bhutan, Cambodia, India, the Philippines. I went up to St. Petersburg, then China. I got tired of traveling. Of the feeling of being always, immanently, and unstoppably in motion. I've been away for so long I don't belong to any one place anymore. I'm like an object, you know? Untethered from the world, identifying with nothing, floating alone through the vast void and its infinite possibilities.

I'm sad. I've been told it's posttravel depression. What a notion. I've been back for nearly a year, though I've barely left the house. In a manner of speaking, of course. I go to the market and, once in a while, to a bookstore-café. I've become friendly with Carla, we chat sometimes. She recommends books, asks how I'm doing. She actually recommends books according to my mood. I've started reading again. Remember how I hadn't been reading much? Our last conversation was about Beckett. I still hold the same feelings as regards his writing and as regards our conversation about him. I remember it took you months to read "First Love"—you said that was how it was meant to be read, through several months, even though it was a really short book. I read it in a single afternoon. And Ana, that's how I've lived my days and my loves, in the space of an afternoon—exotic, aloof, absent, morbid; me and them, we're all the same. Do you think this nausea plagues me for no reason? No, it comes with all the disgust and guilt I feel for God knows what reason, though I suspect it has something to do with my upbringing, you know? My repressed upbringing. I'm not sure I believe all this myself, I'm not sure I believe in anything. I have to connect with my senses, Ana. But how am I supposed to do this when I feel nothing? Nothing moves me, you know? I've even stopped taking photos, stopped driving, stopped writing. We've all got stories and perspectives. What makes mine any different from anyone else's? Why am I capable, deserving, able, while others equally or more talented than me aren't? Why? I ask myself and then feel an enormous sadness. You know? An unceasing thing that creeps up the inner walls of my organs, up and up, and exerts a Kafkian pressure on my esophagus, in my skull, then leaves through my nose and eye sockets in the form of a sweet, exhilarating gas, after which I transmute into nothingness. Ana, I can't stand myself anymore. Something has got to give, something has got to move me, you know? I can't carry on living this way. To be clear: I'm not interested in killing myself, far from it, I'm too self-involved. I just want to *live*, you know? I don't want this garbage lesser-than life, this cute middle-class apartment that just makes me angrier at myself. I know, I know, everything, absolutely everything has its start in the person. But what could possibly begin with me? It's like in Elis Regina's "Brincadeira de Roda." Memory. What do I desire?

I'm writing because I still love you. With no expectations for a response.

This is a desire. Not a cry for help, not my soul reaching out, none of that. Just a desire, begun.

Love,
M.

To: hermeticdramaturge2666@gmail.com

nausea

Hey,

Why would I not answer your email? It's been such a long time since we last talked, it's been forever, and I miss you. I know you're busy and everything, but fuck, you're always running away. Which makes things difficult. I won't ever stop talking to you, but your email worries me. You started by saying you were teaching and that you wanted to discuss something with me and then you forget to mention your classes! I'm curious! What're you teaching? Can I come? Lol. I've got to keep things short for now, a student's just walked in. But I'm here for you, kay? I'll write back when I have more time. And if you want, write again and we'll make plans.

Love,
Ana

p.s. I'd rather see you. That's a desire!

To: talk2anubispipi@gmail.com

nausea

I forgot to talk about the class! Do you see what state I'm in? So, I mentioned the bookstore-café, that's where I'm teaching. It's not exactly a class so much as a film club. We meet to talk about movies. The club already existed, but then the owner of the bookstore—I think she felt sorry for me—asked if I would lead the discussions and, in her words, "validate opinions."

It's been good, you know? Ephemeral. The movies are a mixed bag and so are the participants. It's mostly the seniors who keep coming back. I lied when I said I hadn't been interacting with anyone. I've been interacting with them. After our discussions, they always treat me to coffee and chocolate, and they call me "menina." Menina, Ana! *Young lady.* Which I'm definitely not anymore. Sometimes, I find myself thinking about the metaphysics of progress, of our bodies' journey, you know? Of ways to abstain from practical lives filled with dread and flowers. We talk and say obscene things, but there's nothing to sustain it, nothing can bear the weight of lived experience. I see it in their faces, in every wrinkle that's yet to be etched on my face and may never be. The battle is being waged inside me. And it's impossible to express.

I wanted to delete this email, but it seemed unfair to keep you in the dark about what I was thinking as I thought of you, as I wrote you, even if it's all useless in the end, even if all these words come from a place unknown to me, where they sprout like mushrooms in moisture. I've been thinking of myself as place, you know? The body as place? The body as metaphor for a place traveled, or a life's cartography—with all its marks, signposts, and islands. It's not an exact analogy—the brain's not the city's cultural center and the stomach isn't the gastronomical center—it's a chaotic, borderless map where streets end in dark, narrow alleyways and where our fingers linger in places that are bitter scented and moist. Like our eyes. My eyes are dark, narrow alleyways and I can't see beyond that wall or corner. Now and then, a cat pads in and sits mewing on a dusty windowsill. But I don't pay any attention to it. I'm tired. Nothing's possible, nothing beyond discussions about *Wings of Desire* with seniors who don't get Wim Wenders. You'll say I'm being biased, elitist, that I shouldn't underestimate my interlocutors, but *crois-moi*, darling, they're incapable of it. I'm incapable. I think there was a time when I used to have friends. I don't have many left. You disappear and hope people will stay there, in the world, for you. Like unmoving ports lying in wait for a rudderless boat adrift at sea, and no lighthouse in sight. But you're my *âme soeur*, if you'll forgive the mawkishness, not my port. A sensitive soul mate, virtual in every sense. One drama or another, one cliché or another, takes part in it, and since there isn't much left for us, I think one possible course of action is to say it over and over again, ad infinitum. To get through that turbulent thing we call life. And I'm not saying I think there's something on the other side, I just want to make sense of what is ahead, you know? Because you can't turn back, time marks you, it marked my seniors and it's marked me, too. Though apparently not hard enough, considering they still call me menina. Menina!

I've been feeling so sad. You, who know me and whom I've always looked up to: Have I always been this sad?

Love,
M.

To: talk2anubispipi@gmail.com

nausea

Dearest, everything's awful. Kidding! I bet you just pictured Roberto Carlos's nasal voice. But everything really is awful, you know? I know what my problem is—that sphinx that faces me as I sidestep. My problem is love, Ana. The problem is loving. It's metaphysical desire. I lied. My last trip was to France. You know how much I love France. While I was there I met Alex and Marie, a totally nuts artist couple. She—a painter and tattoo artist—is stunning. I have one of her pieces on my back, a geometric stippling, but minimal and in shocking colors. Sobering, one of a kind. Alex—a photographer and sculptor—is

Russian. I met the two of them on a solo trip to Provence: I'd wanted to photograph the lavender but ended up going at the wrong time of year, sabotaging myself not only with the whole flower cliché but with my own stupidity. Such a me thing to do. Anyway, you know that website you can use to stay at someone's house instead of a hotel? Well, I ended up at the house of these two intense, heady humans. But instead of staying for a week, I stayed for three months. We fell in love, all three of us. You know what I'm like—three-ways and other unconventional relationships pursue me or I pursue them, too, in any case, Ana, it was breezy, subtle, intense. We've got to live these sorts of entanglements now and then—you know what I mean? Till we hit a wall. Three months later, on a chilly morning, I went out for a walk and never looked back. I left everything, Ana. Every single thing. I took my passport and credit card, walked to the train station, bought a ticket, went to the Lyon airport, took a flight to Paris, another from Paris to Lisbon, and then one from Portugal to Brazil. Next thing I knew, I'd gone for an exceedingly long walk. I arrived home, the key was in the planter, what a ridiculous thing it is to leave your key in a planter in the hallway. The doorman opened the door to the building. I went in, took a shower, lay down. I lay down and cried for how love grows into distance. Can you believe it? After two days of being back, Alex called me and I picked up. He was shocked to hear my voice and yelled something to Marie in Russian, some awful thing I'll never know. I didn't feel like explaining anything to him, Ana, not at all. I heard Marie crying, screaming about how worried they were. They started calling me ten, twenty times a day, they said they wanted to come to Brazil, and finally Marie asked me if I was pregnant. I wasn't pregnant, Ana, I've never been. And they started insisting on the insane and paranoid idea of an abortion. They asked why I'd gotten an abortion, then said they would take care of the child, that they wanted to. Ana, I was never pregnant. I just wanted to leave, to walk away, to leave behind this life that wasn't mine, so that's what I did. Do you think it was strange of me to flee like that? Do you, Ana? I don't know, maybe *flee* isn't the right word. I've felt queasy, Ana. Starting a few months after I got back, I felt queasy, it's been about four months now. But I'm sure I'm not pregnant. Not by them, anyway, or the baby would be very overdue. I'm just sad and sick of life.

I haven't been lying about everything. I really do host this film club. But you see, Ana, I can't talk about this sort of thing with them. They're much more interested in treating me to chocolate, tea, lavish slices of cake. I've even gained weight, which is good. That last trip left me looking ill, now I look way more alive, flush. These are the words they use to describe my transformation. They're so sweet. Carla, too. But I'm still shaken by Marie. I'm not attracted to Alex. I can have sex with men, but I never fall for them the way I do for women. Marie is an extravagant woman with short, sweeping hair that grows indomitably up and out and staid, watchful eyes. Slow-motion eyes.

Alex just came with the package. A scam. Sometimes things are complicated that way, they nearly always are for me. I don't think Marie could have kids, and Alex was tired of playing at being an artist, so he wanted to start playing at being a dad. I caught him blackmailing Marie, threatening to leave if she didn't give him a kid, but she couldn't and she told me so with her staid eyes. I caved. I said I'd get pregnant. But I'm no fool. I lied. Isn't that what people do for love? I wanted Marie all to myself, if only just for a little while, if only for a day. I lie all the time. Too much. I lied about going off the pill. I wasn't going to become pregnant, not even by an act of God—if God even exists. But they still think I can. They might even come all the way here just to slap me in the face. A Franco-Russian slap. I wouldn't mind getting slapped around by Marie. For her, I'd get pregnant. But not Alex. I had a serious conversation with Marie and asked her if she wanted to be with me and only me. At first she said no, and then, when I used the pregnancy as bait, she lied, too, and said yes. And Alex lied when he said he'd stay with Marie if she gave him a kid. He's too selfish. We all are. No one's innocent. But now, here I am, with this queasiness that won't let up, distrustful of love. With no one to idolize, not even anyone to tell this story to. A story that could very well become a screenplay for a feature film or an absurdist play, and which would end with Alex and Marie pounding on my apartment door, ready to smack me. A slap in the face. Then, they would kiss my belly. She would kiss my belly, take me in with her eyes, then tear the baby from my flesh. And Alex would walk in, agitated, take a seat on my sofa, and ask if there was anything to drink. But life's not like that, is it, Ana? I must seem crazy to you, telling you my whole story like this, over email, but the thing is, all I've got the strength to do is to talk and talk. You know? To empty my head, drain my strength, hollow myself out. I feel so full. Full of sadness. Literally full up. And this ink, these shapes—all of Marie's artistic prowess on my back—are a symbol, an emblem, a monument. These wings—part human, part stain—that sweep down my arms, weighing on me, they're heavy, Ana. They don't promote flight. No, they bury me, pin my body to the ground with their absolute weight. And you know what, ever since I had them done, meaning ever since Marie gave me these wings, I've felt the world shifting beneath my feet, strange and slow, like her eyes. A minute, inescapable movement. I feel like a puppet bowing under the weight of these drawn wings, or maybe from the jadedness of the hands that hold me.

I'm jaded.

You're probably sick of my grumbling.

I'm sorry, Ana. You don't have to answer. I won't write again.

To: hermeticdramaturge2666@gmail.com

!!!!!!

M. for Menina!

You've always been melancholic, poetic, and a little sad, too, but a lovely kind of sad. The sadness of a moon dappled between the blossoms of an orange tree. Remember? It was a long time ago. We were at the country house of a friend you had back then. You were always switching friend groups, but I never saw it as a bad thing. The truth is I envied you.

Oh, you just sent another email! I'm going to read it, then I'll finish writing—just so it's on the record! =)

I'm sort of confused. I've read your other email. I didn't delete what I wrote before because of what you said about not deleting things after they were written—anyway, I didn't think it was fair. But . . . I'm confused.

I don't know what to do, if I should ask direct questions, or if you just want to talk. I'm not even sure I should be asking any questions at all. And now you're saying I don't have to answer. Wait a second, I think

I've got a right to answer. And my answer is I need you to send me your phone number, right now. I want to talk to you. I tried your old number, but it's not working. Another thing, do you still live in the same place? Can I stop by tomorrow? When's good for you? I want to see you, and I get the sense you need to talk, so maybe we should bring these two desires together. What do you say? Write back with the best time and I'll come by tomorrow. Or Wednesday? I don't want to intrude or anything, but I can come by today, if you want, even at night. It doesn't matter, okay? You can count on me. Always. I'll wait for you to email back.

To: talk2anubispipi@gmail.com

nausea

I'm afraid I can't let you come by, I can't meet you, I can't even see you. It's not that I don't want to, I just can't. Ana, I can't. But let me reassure you with this piece of news: yesterday, I started writing a play. Yep. I hadn't written a thing in years, and all of a sudden, yesterday, it came to me, volcanic—surge after surge of scenes, actions, dilemmas. I've even got the lighting figured out. I've thought of everything. And I want your honest opinion. I'm not attaching the document—I want to finish it first—but here's the story.

A woman can't leave her house to go to work. There's a leaky faucet in the kitchen. The drip gets louder and louder, stronger and stronger, unceasing, uninterrupted. It seeps into all her thoughts. All of a sudden, she starts repeating certain motions in sync with the sound of the faucet. Realizing, she fastens a dish towel around the metal pipe to stanch the drip. Minutes later, the dish towel is drenched. The silence is broken by the faucet, which once again begins to dribble. It's unbearable. We discover that she can't leave the house because she is locked in. That morning, her husband has taken her key by mistake and left on a business trip. There's been a power cut in the neighborhood, so her cell phone is dead. She can't call a locksmith. The intercom's broken. The play takes place on a Monday morning. At first, our character thinks she'll be fired, that she'll never be excused for something so stupid. That morning, which would have otherwise been any other ordinary morning—had she not locked herself in the house—her anxieties bubble to the surface. The stage lighting is the sun shining through the window, providing a sense of passing time. The piece ends when the power comes back and the protagonist forgets all her suffering and stops questioning herself. Once the power's back, she takes her key from her purse, as if she'd always known it was there, unlocks the door, and leaves for work as if nothing at all happened. But there's still that one latent nuisance, represented by the water's unceasing dribble.

What do you think?

Now that I've reread it, I see how stupid the plot is. Ana, I'm not sure what I'm doing, I can't write anymore.

I could write a piece about the Cunhas and the Canallis, two couples whose kids had a run-in in the park. One had knocked the other's teeth out with a stick, because they hadn't been welcomed by the other's group of friends. The play would unfold in the Cunha family's erudite, well-to-do living room, which is chock full of books and art, and where they sip coffee and eat apple pie until, all of a sudden, the conversation stops making sense and a volley of insults and vomit ensues. But Yasmina Reza has already written this story and Polanski's already adapted it into a movie. We discussed it at the club last week, and all people could talk about was how children were being brought up these days. So, I'm stuck with the story of the woman who can't leave her house because of a stupid faucet.

Can you see the difference, Ana? I'm a maker of failures.

Did you like it?

I'll be away for the next few months, I'm going to Germany. When I'm back, if I really do come back, I'll call and you can come over for coffee on a Wednesday.

Yours always and forever,
M.

p.s. I changed the subject line to "nausea" again because those exclamation marks made me uncomfortable.

Mute: hermeticdramaturge2666@gmail.com

COMO TE EXTRAÑO, CLARA

Fernanda leaves the parking lot with a knot that travels from her neck to her belly. And back. She almost pukes some three times before reaching the first traffic light, which is red. Eduardo's name blinks on her cell phone screen as Aretha Franklin, her voice muffled by the leather upholstery, sings, "Ain't gonna do you wrong while you're gone." Fernanda doesn't pick up and the phone goes silent at *A-N-S*. Before the light changes, she looks at her classwork scattered on the back seat. Tidiness, another promise she can't keep. The light turns and Aretha starts up again. Rolling her eyes, Fernanda feels around the seat for her phone. This time, Clara's name glows onscreen.

"Hey."

"Hi. Just wanted to say I already miss you."

Fernanda smiles and says she misses her, too. They both have class—Fernanda, at university; Clara, at culinary school—so they arrange to see each other some other day. Traffic is slow and a muggy heat has begun to grip the city. It's a strange Thursday. Fernanda hangs up. The knot creeps back up her throat and, this time, does not come down. She remains still, suffocating. She knows she won't keep her promise.

Fernanda and Clara met in civil engineering: Fernanda, the professor; Clara, the student. Not exactly the model student but an enthralling person. Clara worked at one of the university cafés.

"I kept seeing you around the building, so I decided to work there."

"Pity I don't teach industrial automation."

"Seriously, you could've saved me the trouble of acing engineering just to meet you."

"Well, aren't you daring."

"Have you just noticed?"

"Speaking of, we've got to be careful in class, people might notice. I think they might already suspect something. But I'm not entirely sure."

"Well, you're always calling on me to answer."

"True. I don't even know why. Next thing I know, your name's on my lips."

"It's the eye thing."

"What eye thing?"

"Something I've had since school."

"Not that long ago, then."

"Yeah, yeah, smart-ass, except as far as I know, I've had it since fifth grade."

"So what's the eye thing?"

"It's like this. Whenever I want a teacher to call on me, I look at them, but without coming off as desperate or anything. Just to show them I'm there, and I'm listening, that I know what I'm talking about. It's a passing look that goes like this." Her eyes scanned Fernanda's eyes, then looked away, at some slow-moving point, and back—again scanning Fernanda's eyes. "It can't appear desperate or bitter. It's got to be coy."

"How does it go again? Show me one more time."

"All right, sit over there on the edge of the bed."

Fernanda went. She sat against the headboard, her arms resting on her dark thighs and hands on her knees.

"There."

"Now ask the class something."

"Right. Does anyone have anything they want to say about environmental preservation?"

Clara did the eye thing.

"Clara?"

"See!"

And they laughed and kissed.

The traffic gets worse. Her tardiness is now less a possibility than a certainty. Every time she gives Clara a ride, she's late. Thursday is the only day Rafael has after-school support, and Eduardo has lunch with his work colleagues in the afternoon.

Which means that the house is empty at noon, and she can be with Clara. With husband and son out, the house is theirs.

Clara and Fernanda have been seeing each other for a year and eight months. In the beginning, they went for coffee off campus, later to restaurants, then to the library, and finally Fernanda suggested they meet at her house. Every Thursday, Clara has Spanish at one thirty, and when she doesn't cut class, Fernanda drives her. Lessons are held in a building in the center of town. Parking's impossible there at that time of day, so they drive into the parking lot and sit around for fifteen minutes until, finally, Clara is late.

Clara told Fernanda she loved her, and Fernanda said: "I love you, too, Clara."

"Then leave your husband. Be with me."

Fernanda closed her eyes, letting her lungs fill with air. As the air shifted the thoughts arranged in her chest and in her head, she tried to make sense of the last couple of developments in her life. But nothing seemed to want to settle down in the appropriate place, someplace where it was less burdensome and wouldn't get in the way of fate's other plans. Her life had reached a nerve center, a point so knotted it could only be fixed by slicing through it—untangling it just wasn't an option.

"You don't have to say anything. That was silly of me. I'm sorry. I know I don't have the right to ask anything of you."

Fernanda didn't say a word. She just smiled and, as Clara got out of the car, kissed her. Then she turned on the engine and drove out of the parking lot.

"I won't take money from you, Dona Fernanda, you were only in there for a few minutes. You can head on out."

"Thanks, Gentil."

No one seems to want to demand anything from Fernanda. Still, she feels indebted and racks her brain for ways to make up for it. Christmas hampers for Seu Gentil and Clara. Or for Clara, maybe something a little less concrete.

Fernanda has been parked on the same road for eight minutes. Gazing at herself in the rearview mirror, she thinks to herself that she really is beautiful: a flood of brown hair curling sinuously around her cheekbones, thick eyelashes that give her an unceasingly dramatic look, a constant quiver in lips that arch naturally down. As she smiles, a small sigh slips out the corner of her mouth. Her desire to justify her circumstances with well-constructed arguments that have no bearing on the truth makes her feel ridiculous. She loves Clara. She is in love. Eduardo is the shadow of a life that she stubbornly clings onto. Before Clara, there was Luciana, a huge disappointment. Luciana was even more frightened than Fernanda, and neither would ever speak of what happened. It was only once, on a winter evening. There were no memories, no explanations. Luciana moved to another state, Fernanda regretted it for years. Then Eduardo arrived on scene.

The cars start moving faster. She opens the window and a festive breeze blows through the car, whirling behind her. The city is in the grips of a clammy fog come from God only knows where with no intention to leave. For a second, she wonders if the fog came from inside her. The evening blackens. A storm brews. It's chaos. Everyone's desperate to reach their destinations as swiftly as possible. Elevators become overcrowded, awnings seem to shrink in size, and the faces of passersby dashing down streets and sidewalks darken in dismay. Nobody wants to get wet. Not even those who checked the weather forecast, not even those who saw those gloomy clouds gathering in that corner of the world, not even them. A scant few don't mind, their moods remaining unchanged. Still, most would rather not spend the rest of the day with damp hemlines and damp feet, not even the ones carrying umbrellas.

Fernanda's thoughts are dulled by a truck crashing into the driver's door. Whirl. The wind dances around her head. She catches her reflection in the rearview mirror. Blood drenched, her hair forms a sinuous curve, a lovely reddish loop around her left temple. She can't move her arms. She closes her eyes. She feels a sharp pressure in her neck and hears voices mingling. She opens her eyes. A bright light. She closes her eyes. Things take on the hackneyed swiftness of life. Into the ambulance.

"Clara."

"Fernanda. Your name is Fernanda, right? Look at me, Fernanda. We've called your husband."

The emergency contact on her phone. Eduardo.

"He's on his way."

"Clara."

Fernanda has a concussion. Her left arm and forearm are broken in three places. She's also broken her clavicle. A truck sped through a light and rammed into her.

It's Friday morning by the time Fernanda wakes up. Eduardo and Rafael are there.

"Headphones out, kid, Mom's awake."

"Hey. What happened?"

"A truck hit you at the light. Totaled your pickup. I'm not sure how you weren't killed."

"Mom, can I take a photo of you for Insta?"

"What? No, Rafael."

"Fine, I'll delete it, but it's gotten, like, almost a hundred likes."

Fernanda doesn't mind or understand or give any thought to it at all.

"Where's my cell?"

"Here."

"Hand it over."

"No."

Eduardo sits quietly. He stares at Fernanda. His head is brimming. All the messages mixing with a reality that appears disjointed. He thinks of Clara.

"My cell, please."

Through clenched teeth, Eduardo says: "Clara called."

Fernanda shuts her eyes again. Her head aches. She slowly opens her eyes. Eduardo continues.

"Clara texted. I'll read it for you. 'Why aren't you saying anything? You're online. I didn't mean to pressure you, I still love you. Nothing has to change.'"

Fernanda continues to stare at the window. Rafael, with his headphones in, begrudgingly deletes his post.

"Will you hand me my cell already?"

"Don't you have anything to say to me?"

Fernanda stays silent.

"Is that all?"

Eduardo chucks the phone on the bed and walks out.

"Where did Dad go?"

"I'm not sure, Rafael. I think he went to find something to eat."

"Cool, I'm hungry."

There's nothing Fernanda can do. Maybe this is what life is like. Depending on the choice you make, there's no way back, and the path Fernanda has taken until then doesn't leave room for Clara. This is what goes through her head.

Rafael frames his mother in the background of a selfie he posts with the hashtags *#hospitalwithmamis #accident #totalloss*. Fernanda wonders what she will do without Eduardo, what she'll do about Rafael. She wonders what will become of all the ordered things in her life if she chooses to take another path. Then she wonders if she's getting ahead of herself—she doesn't exactly know what the situation is, she isn't even sure if Clara actually wants to do what she said she did. She wonders whether she'd rather play another part in the ridiculous drama her life has been until that moment. And under her breath, she says, *"Como te extraño, Clara."* Because everything is dark and strange in the too-small perhaps-possibility of this life change, too brittle, like her bones after the car crash. She doesn't know what shape all these new, dangerous, and alluring things unfolding before her will take.

Clara only comes on Monday. Eduardo has already packed up all his stuff and left, without ceremony. He is hurt, his pride shattered. He can never tell anyone that his wife cheated on him with a younger student—a woman. No. Fernanda understands. But the apparent ease with which he took his stuff and left the house seems to suggest that the dissatisfaction was mutual. Rafael wasn't surprised. He is an apathetic teenager—or maybe just a normal one.

Clara rushes into the room and, not noticing the boy, tries to kiss Fernanda, who quickly turns her cheek but still hugs her as hard as she can with one arm. Midhug, Clara spots Rafael, with his headphones in, chuckling at his cell phone screen.

"What happened? I was convinced you never wanted to see me again. I don't know, I thought that, you know, I thought I'd done something wrong. And you weren't answering your phone, I was terrified, I wasn't sure I'd ever see you again.

Then I heard about that awful accident. What happened? I was scared to death, *meu amor*, *meu amor*, I don't know what to say. I'm so happy you're all right."

"Eduardo's gone."

"I don't know, I didn't see him."

"I'm not asking, Clara. He's gone. He read our messages. I think he read everything. On my cell, for sure. But also our emails and everything else afterward, too, I think."

"No—how?"

"I leave everything on at home, all my passwords are saved. He just has to sign in and read."

"But," she chokes, "now what?"

"This. The two of us. Me, broken, you with that terrified look on your face. And the kid."

Clara feels such a potent mix of happiness and fear that she sheds a couple of tears. Fernanda is still in shock from the accident, the events. Rafael is engrossed in the likes and comments for the photo he took of his banged-up mom in the hospital bed.

On Tuesday, before Spanish class, Clara will walk past the parking lot and Seu Gentil will ask her about Fernanda. Clara will say that Fernanda is well and that she'll be up and running again soon enough, and the man will say he's sorry to hear about her mom, that she's a good, hardworking woman. Clara won't get it at first. She will know that this man has never met her mother and that there is nothing the matter with her. Five steps later, she'll realize he's talking about Fernanda. For the first time, Clara will think of how old Fernanda is, and in a quick calculation, she will realize that the man's assumption is not unreasonable, although it is reductive, which annoys her. She will walk up to her Spanish class, on the tenth floor, and that afternoon, she will learn nothing. On that same Tuesday, Rafael will ask his mother if Clara will be moving in with them. It will take a moment for Fernanda to make sense of his question. He'll try to help by saying, "Clara, Mom, your girlfriend," with unusual ease. Aretha Franklin will start singing, "What you want, babe, I got it. What you need, do you know I got it? All I'm asking is for a little—" as Clara's name blinks on the broken cell phone screen.

MARÍLIA WAKES UP

She wears knee-length socks because her feet are cold even in summer. She sits on the edge of the bed and rolls them down—shin, calf, ankle—then stops. She rights herself. Her stomach stops her from bending over. She takes a deep breath, stretches her arms, and finishes the job. She folds her socks and places them under her pillow. They're for sleeping. Marília may not be sweet, but gazing at her from the other half of our bed, I can't help loving her.

There goes Marília into the kitchen, and I think of how I will soon be roused by the sound of metal clanging, drawers closing, and the whistling of an old tune we no longer know the lyrics to. I face the window, its blinds still shadowy from twilight, close my eyes, and smile. The racket begins. She doesn't do it on purpose, her hands just don't know silence. The door slams, and from the depths of our home, I hear the same old melody. I wonder what song it is. I figure it must be ours.

I know that soon I'll have to pretend I'm fast asleep, because Marília will return to bed with coffee and some toast and, time permitting, a flower penned on a napkin. Marília likes remote-controlled cars, clothespins, skirts with pockets, and plants. She would never, ever pluck a flower. So she draws them.

The door opens. Marília sits on our bed, without the tray. She touches my leg, and I pretend to have just woken up. Her silhouette is drawn by the now-bright window blinds. I hold her jittery hands and know that something is wrong before even opening my eyes. I ask what the matter is. She tells me she is forgetful. I say we are. She looks at me gloomily and says she made coffee without the grounds and burned the toast. I scrunch up my forehead in confusion. She repeats that she brewed the coffee without the grounds, so there was only boiling water in the coffeepot, and as she poured the water into the coffee mugs, she stood quietly for a moment, perplexed. Which was when the toast burned. She tells me she's old and forgetful. I say we're two forgetful old ladies.

I look at her hair, now on my lap. She lies on her side and asks me to cover her feet, "Just my feet," she says, and open the windows. I stretch my back and arms until I reach the cord for the blinds. The light unveils us: my blemished hands on her white hair. How many years has it been, Marília? How long have we been carrying on this Sunday-morning ritual? I think, but I say nothing. Marília seems to be crying a little. If so, it's on the inside. She tells me she's going to get breakfast ready. She gets up and walks away.

No flower this time, I see. I don't dare ask why. I sip my coffee slowly so that I don't burn my chapped lips. I take small bites of my bread so as not to choke on any harder bits. Marília eats too, her gaze down. A new bashfulness has risen between us. I finish. I look out the window again. It's a lovely day. I feel like taking a walk around our yard. Marília stands up and places the paddle walker beside the bed. She knows I want to get up by myself, and I do. Though there are only a few stairs, they still give me trouble. Still, I don't want an elevator in the house and I can't stand the thought of a wheelchair ramp. Marília opens the door and we walk out into the morning light. It's colder than I anticipated. She grabs a knit blanket we've had forever and drapes it on my back. She gives my shoulders a hard squeeze with her clunky hands; she still hasn't figured out the exact amount of affection to extend after all these years. I like it. Because I know our love is contained in that act, in that force. And we stand there, behind the wall that shelters our backyard from the street, that shelters our lives from passersby.

Two old women live there, in that house. They've been living there for years, those two old women. There's something about those two old women who've been living there together for years. There, in the house of those two odd old women.

We're two odd old women, Marília and I. And as I think of us, the sun glides past the orange tree and starts to warm my head, a bit too much. I try to get up. My legs lost their strength from night to day, and I never found out why. I went to doctors, magicians, healers, but none of it was any use, I never got the strength back. And I was the one who used to enjoy taking long walks, walking around the neighborhood, hiking in the woods, up the hills, by waterfalls—why me? Now I can barely get across my own patio. So I just sit quietly on the lawn, five steps from the chair I was sitting in before, because I find it hard to balance. I glance back at the house. I can't spot Marília. I can't stand and I start to feel anxious, but then she emerges from behind the pillar and asks if I'm all right, if I fell, did I hurt myself, and runs clunkily to help me. Before she reaches me, I tell her I'm fine and invite her to sit on the grass. She grumbles about the dew but sits down anyway. Grumpily, she tells me I'll catch cold, but still she stays. She pats my leg a bit too hard, which I take to mean she loves me and that she's sorry about everything. I smile and say I want to go in, even though I don't really. I go because I know she wants to.

Marília likes routines. On Sundays, she gets up early and makes us breakfast. Then we sit on the front porch for a while. If there's sunshine, we sit in the yard. After this, she likes to go inside and read the paper. On Sunday mornings, I used to go for walks, but now I sit and read the paper too. We eat, then we nap, then we watch TV, then we eat again. Then, before going to bed, we look at each other for a very long time. We look at each other so that we can try and understand how on earth we got to this point. We never do. We always do. We are very quiet; we've always enjoyed silence.

Marília is helping me bathe. She washes my back with her rickety hands. She is still ashamed of our bodies. Or maybe it is this new, age-old bashfulness. She shampoos my head three times, and I can tell there's something wrong, but I don't say a word. I'm scared. It's fair for me to be scared. But it would be unfair of me to show her my fear. Marília is constantly afraid of everything. She may seem tough, but on the inside, she's scared to death. For my part, I'm still and once again scared, and every day I pray we will die together, because I couldn't bear to be on my own, nor could she. I've thought of taking care of it myself. Of doing it quietly, of getting into bed with Marília, in her sleeping socks, and mixing something soothing into our nighttime tea. Hopefully we would never wake up. I've only ever thought about it, though; I don't have the courage. So I pray. I pray we'll be together, as together as we've always been, now and at the hour of our death.

The following Sunday, Marília wakes up, then wakes me up with the scent of coffee, the sound of drawers closing, and our wordless tune.

LESBIAN DIASPORA

Chica still hadn't arrived. As we waited, we decided to have a few laughs at her expense.

L: Girls, where's Chica?

J: Probably putting her leotard on.

P: Ay. What's up with the sudden interest in leotards, hey? They don't suit her at all, with those blackheads all over her back. Someone's gotta tell her, for the love of God.

L: You tell her, you're, like, close and all.

P: Not me! Jesus.

Juli knew everything. Juli always knew everything. She had a lot of social cachet and often went out with both groups. She shed some light on the mystery: Chica was dating a straight woman, a socialite, so she was supposed to make an effort.

P: Fine, but someone please tell her that the kind of effort she's making isn't working. Am I the only one who thinks the leotards and floral shirts have upped her dykeyness?

We all laughed in agreement. Lea asked if the so-called socialite would be joining her today, but Juli said no. Preta nodded at Tânia to bring over the menus.

P: I don't know about you guys, but I'm in need of a beer.

B: I'm up for something stronger.

It was the first time Bea had opened her mouth. She and her girlfriend were in a crappy mood on account of some misunderstanding earlier in the supermarket. Purple lettuce. Iceberg lettuce. And they were out of sorts with each other.

P: Drink up, *amor*. Maybe that'll make us less obnoxious.

B: Glad you've included yourself.

Bea and Preta were a baffling couple. But they deserved each other. An open relationship, perfect and lively. Any jealousy was incidental. Once, Preta had ogled a straight couple in a bar—though she'd actually just been staring into space—and Bea hadn't thought twice before kicking up a stink. No way in hell was she going to sleep with them, she exclaimed. Preta didn't understand what was going on, and Bea became increasingly hysterical. Until, without thinking, Preta slapped her across the face, got up, and walked right out. That same evening, they made up and had makeup sex. Now, at the table, they ordered two shots of Captain Morgan each. They had a long night ahead of them. Which would probably only end once they'd dived into a hotel pool and, the next morning, into the hotel's breakfast buffet.

L: You all wanna hear some lesbian drama?

P: What a ridiculous question. Course we do.

L: Inês is back in town . . . and she's single.

J: Hell no! Wasn't Inês married and living up north with some chick from Vitória?

L: Yep, last I heard they'd started a frozen foods business.

B: Guys, having Inês back in town is terrifying.

P: Ayay. Crossing myself in case she shows up.

J: Don't even joke about that.

Inês was a predator. When attached, she was a recluse, but whenever her relationships ended, God help everyone, because Inês went on the hunt. And hunt she did. She shot women down and took them home. She was always messing people up. Last time she'd come out with our group, she'd told everyone she was seeing someone. She'd made a point of saying so because we were with Juli, who'd managed to shake Inês loose after a great deal of persistence. She told everyone she was moving away, like meeting someone and moving across the country for them was no biggie. The relationship had lasted three years. Now she was back, painting the town red.

B: But why's she back?

L: Well, that's the thing! Looks like she was cheating on the chick from Vitória with a sixteen-year-old she met on Leskut.

P: Is Leskut even a thing anymore?

J: Apparently, people have gone back to it 'cause Brenda's too mainstream.

L: Girls, Inês hooked up with a teenager, and all you can talk about is Leskut? For fuck's sake, what is *wrong* with this country?

B: I'm scared to death of that *punani*. She nearly swung at me once. At a Shoes gig.

P: Oh, I *love* Shoes. They're the best!

B: Yeah, they're so amazing. But anyway, I was staring into space—this happens sometimes, I sort of look through people—and she got it into her head that I had my eyes on her ex, Cica, superlative Cica. Except I didn't. She came at me with hands balled up into fists, and if Cica hadn't grabbed her by the wrist, I would've taken one to the eye. Wouldn't I have, *amor*?

P: Yeah. That dyke is e-vil.

B: Super evil.

J: What about the minor?

The Leskut girl was from São Paulo. Inês had gone there—she'd been sent for work to a trade fair—taken her to a motel, and made her a thousand promises. She went to São Paulo another five times that year, until all of a sudden she just stopped going. The girl, Rita—not her real name, but she was hooked on Ritalin—was hospitalized for attempted suicide. Inês really did mess people up. But what she wasn't expecting when she came home from her last trip to São Paulo was for Rafaela, the chick from Vitória, to have changed the locks and thrown Inês's stuff into storage. After that, it was just trouble:

cops, lawyers, emotional blackmail. Until, to everyone's dismay, Inês gave up.

P: Look, girls, it's Chica.

J: The woman with her, isn't she a celebrity trainer?

B: Ugh, I hate that woman. She's totally ridiculous.

L: Why? Tell us before they get here.

B: Snooty, nose in the air. Wait and see for yourself, you'll understand.

C: Hey, girls.

Everyone: Hey, Chica.

C: This is Aline. Aline, these are Preta, Lea, Julia, Bea, and Zica.

A: Hi.

C: What're you all drinking?

We all raised our glasses.

A: Wow, you're all hardcore, huh? Only hard work and prayer will get that off your thighs. I'll start with some coconut water, I'm on a detox. I'll let you know if it works. Apparently, it does wonders for your skin and your bod. A real miracle worker.

Our faces and glasses dropped; our drinks had soured.

C: I'm having a beer.

A: Chu, are you sure? What about that belly fat, huh, how're you planning to lose that?

J (*to the others, under her breath*): I'll lose my fist in your face.

C: But it's Saturday.

A: Well, it's up to you. So long as you don't go blubbering at me during training or start whining in front of the mirror.

C: Tânia, I'll have a pineapple juice. Hold the sugar.

A: That's my Chu.

B (*looking at Preta*): Chu? Nah, girls.

Everyone burst out laughing.

C: Sweetie, don't call me that in public, okay?

A: I'm sorry! I didn't realize.

From that day forward, Chica would forever be Chu.

P: So what do you do, Aline?

A: Oh my God, I can't believe you don't know me. Tut, tut. I guess you all don't go to the gym or have an Instagram account?

P: No. I go out to bars and events where people, like, actually socialize. I don't imagine you've heard of such things?

L: Girls, who invited Inês?

J: Why?

Everyone glanced at the entrance, where Inês stood waving at the table.

B: Are you serious? Who invited her? Was it you, Chica?

C: Not me.

I: Hey, girls. It's so nice bumping into you here. I thought I'd end up sitting on my lonesome at this old dyke bar. I'm so glad I didn't have to.

L: Yeah, sure.

C: Back in a minute. I'll go fetch your coconut water from the bar, it's taking way too long.

A: Thanks.

I: Grab me a chair while you're at it, will you, Chica!

C (*solicitous*): Okay.

I: So I know everyone here except for you. Hi, I'm Inês.

A: Hi, Inês. Aline.

I: Aline Herrera. The athlete?

A: Yeah, that's right!

I: I follow you on Insta. I adore your health tips and pics of gluten- and lactose-free sweets, your selfies. What a bod.

A: Aw, thanks! It's so cool to meet a fan. (*She cackles like an old hen.*)

We all looked at each other, predicting how the night would end. Chica came back carrying a chair over her naked back. She was wearing a leotard again.

A couple of hours and a couple of drinks later, Inês was shamelessly hitting on Chica's girlfriend, and worst of all, the cheeky bitch was flirting back. We tried not to talk about it, but our expressions quickly changed from laughter to terror. Half of us hit the dance floor once it opened. Chica, Juli, and Bea stayed at the table.

J: Chica, can't you see Inês is hitting on Aline? Are you blind or something?

B: That dyke is evil and your woman is no straight shooter either. I'm sorry, but it's true. I don't like her.

C: Nah, Aline's like that with everyone. She's a public figure, she's got to be nice to people.

J: Since when does having an Instagram account make someone a public figure? Wake up, Chica. She's gonna fool around on you.

C: Maybe . . . do you think?

B: If I were you, I'd be on the dance floor right now.

Chica went to the back of the bar. It was dark and it took a while for her eyes to adjust to the neon lights. Preta and Lea waved at her. The music was loud, the lights fast, the scent of booze sharp, and people were dancing frenetically.

C: Where's Aline?

P: Huh?

C: Where's Aline?

P: At the table!

C: No, she isn't there!

L: She went to sit down, like, five minutes ago, maybe ten.

C: And Inês?

P: At the bar, or in the bathroom. Dunno.

Chica gripped her head with both hands, then elbowed her way to the bathroom. She didn't have to try hard to find them: they were making out by the sink. Aline looked away, Inês smiled. Chica went back to the table, grabbed her things, and left. Juli chased after her.

C: I'm going to kill that *puta*.

J: Which one?

C: Both of them.

J: Hon, they're made for each other. Aline is an idiot, and Inês, well, no comment. Rebounds are always like that. Unbelievable.

Juli was right. We all gathered at the street corner where Juli and Chica were sitting. That was, except for Aline and Inês, who checked into a hotel that same night. None of us were huge fans of Chica, either, but it was a moment of sisterhood.

L: Look at the bright side, Chica. No one'll ever call you Chu again, Eshu.

Everybody laughed and thought that really was a positive, because a couple with a nickname like that was bad news.

L: Another thing, while we're at it. Enough already with those ridiculous leotards. I beg you. Seriously, that woman was going through you fast.

C: Do you really hate the leotards?

P: And the makeup. Too much.

J: And your nails. Uh-gly.

C: Would you not have mentioned any of this if I were still with Aline?

Everyone: Maybe.

Or we might've just found a new haunt. For months, Chica came out with us. Until she and Aline got back together, and out came the leotards and the excessive makeup. A pity, we all agreed. Inês was still out there, pulling stunts in bars across town. We started staying in. Eventually, Tânia's closed, kicking off a lesbian diaspora that affected several nightclubs in the area.

AMORA

Another medal on her chest: junior state chess champion. She looked down at the golden biscuit conferring her a title beyond her age. After three consecutive years, this was going to be the last time Amora would win first place. Earlier that same day, she'd met Júnior. During the break between one game and the next, she chatted with him in the gym mezzanine. They discussed the chances of winning that championship and found out they lived in the same city, actually in bordering neighborhoods, and each thought of how tiny the world was, though full of surprises, and finally, Amora felt a small itch spread through her belly. When it rose, her heartbeats went awry and the hairs on the back of her neck froze into pins; when it fell, the itch turned into flickering fires and memories of damp springs, sweat, softness, and flowers. When Amora got home that evening, both her heart and medal were gleaming. She told her parents and her siblings about the championship, about the checkmates, and about how she'd managed to win two games with a single pawn. She kept everything she would've said about Júnior to herself. Later, in bed, Amora fell asleep thinking of everything she'd felt that day.

On Saturday around noon, Alexandre and Felipe yelled out to her from the gate to her house. She stuck her head out the window. We're going to play pinball, grab Mateus's bike and come with us. Amora informed her parents, took her brother's bicycle, and, before leaving, shoved her hair in a baseball cap. Off they went, three kids. Be back for lunch, okay? she heard her mother say as she disappeared around the corner. Saturday morning was the best time to go to the arcade. It was always empty and you didn't have to compete for a machine; on top of that, the owner promised everyone extra tokens. But not that day. There was a pinball tournament on and a bunch of the machines were taken. Amora dashed to *Street Fighter* as soon as she saw a boy walk away from it, while Alexandre and Felipe waited in line to play *NBA Jam*. Amora's dash ended with a bashing of shoulders and a jostling for the arcade machine. Winner stayed. Amora spied the person speaking from under her cap. It was Júnior, smiling down at her. Amora smiled back and accepted the challenge. Júnior wasn't as good as she was and had to focus hard on the game, but Amora didn't stop talking for one second. When Amora's Chun-Li knocked out Júnior's Zangief, they both snapped their fingers and looked at one another. Amora smiled and wondered how he could be so pretty and yet such a bad gamer. She would make a joke about it, then invite him out for ice cream that afternoon. But then Júnior asked Amora if she had a sister who played chess. Ice. The pins at the back of her neck bored into her body and toward the fire that licked at her with moist flames, extinguishing it. The air was dry and thick with smoke, and a chunk of hard, cold charcoal soiled everything inside her. A blur. Amora left the arcade without a word, walked to the bikes, and, looking straight ahead of her into the depths of an abyss, cycled away.

When she got home, she dodged her mom and dad and, like a knight moving in an L, went to the bathroom. She gazed at herself in the mirror. Baseball cap, ponytail, an overlong, flat band T-shirt that clung to her body—devoid of the accents of other girls her age—ripped jean shorts, scabbed knee, black flip-flops exposing long, ragged toenails. She chucked her hat on the floor and thought of how Júnior might have recognized her without it.

For eight months, Amora didn't like anyone. Her disappointment with Júnior had hardened her soul. She drew skulls and broken hearts in her notebook and on book jackets. And yet, in those eight months, her body, a straight rook, turned into a queen. As if to protect her mutating girl-woman heart, two small mounds budded on her chest; she was strong, with her medals above them. Amora with tar-black eyes and juicy purplish lips. Amora with painted nails. Delicate Amora, at times sweet or sour, at times harsh, yet always delicate, fluid.

She arrived at the gym in her uniform. The teacher waved. School championship. Júnior leaned on a column beside other boys made awkward by age, a feast of fine white shins and arms that ended in hands so large they looked like they'd drag on the ground. Deep voices. Some were still colts, while others were already horses. Most, though, remained big-headed pawns. He didn't recognize Amora, this time for another reason.

The finals were postponed until the afternoon. Having won all five games in her group, Amora had made it to the finals. The winner of the other group had also won all five games. At the exit to the gym, she noticed the boys talking about her. She ignored them, she was in the zone. She had lunch at a diner in the area but was soon back to go over some moves. She lost track of time. Next thing she knew, they were announcing the tables. Amora and Angélica, table two. She didn't hear Júnior's name. He hadn't made the cut. She went to the table, sat down, and pondered her three opening moves. Looking up, she saw Angélica. Red cheeks, as if scorching hot inside, left arm hanging limply by the board, fingertips drumming impatiently, her other arm wedged between her legs, beneath the table. Amora reached out her right hand to greet her before the match, a formality, but Angélica just dropped her eyes and extended the hand that was moments ago fidgeting with a chess piece. This bothered Amora. Angélica moved her pawn and, with that same hand, hit the chess clock. Amora moved the same pawn, a mirror move, and hit the clock. Three moves later, and Amora thought her opponent must be underestimating her with her pathetic attempt at a scholar's mate. She counterattacked. Angélica started on a Philidor defense. She was sweating, restless in her chair, and, before starting her tenth move, dried off her forehead with her other arm, which ended in a curved stump at the wrist with a fresh, reddish scar. Amora froze, and before she could do anything to stop herself, the words left her mouth. What happened to your arm? I lost my hand in an accident. I was hit by a van, my hand was squashed like a pancake, they couldn't save it. Amora's lunch lurched in her stomach like Angélica's zigzagging bishops. Checkmate. Amora gazed down at the pieces and reached her right hand out to the winner, then checked herself and quickly extended her left. The teacher was surprised by her defeat. Amora wanted to say something about her opponent's pancaked hand but knew that, even though it had really affected her, it was a silly excuse.

There was a long afternoon of awards ahead of them. Amora was sitting in the shade of a trumpet tree when Angélica asked if she could join her. You're really good. You are too. I've never seen you at any competitions, though. I'm from Rio, I moved here two months ago. I could tell from your accent but didn't want to assume. Angélica was holding her arm with her other hand, and though she tried not to look, Amora was mesmerized by the sight. Funny, isn't it? Wanna touch? Yeah.

Amora touched the scar with her fingertips. I can still feel my hand, you know. What do you mean, you can still feel it? I'm not sure. They say it's normal. It's funny, right now it feels like you're holding it. Amora mulled this over. It was strange and lovely, she thought, that they were holding hands. The chunk of charcoal in Amora's belly glowed red with a mix of excitement and embarrassment. Angélica smiled and brushed away a lock of Amora's hair. She sighed. Amora recognized the feeling but didn't get how it could be possible. That afternoon under the trumpet tree, they spoke every possible word to one another.

They received their medals. Amora went home with a silver biscuit on her chest. Her parents were surprised. Then she told them about Angélica, about the accident, and about how her hand felt like it was still attached to her body. Nothing about moves and checkmates. Angélica was the hot topic. She wanted to see her again, to talk to her again, to learn more about her accident and her recovery; she wanted more Angélica. The smell of her perfume still lingered in her nose. Her insides shivered. As she spoke about her, she realized she was already in love with Angélica, even though it hadn't been long. And when she remembered they'd agreed to get ice cream the following weekend, she felt a thrill. Amora counted the days and rushed the minutes until they turned into hours.

It was raining. They met under the green awning of Sorveteria da Kika. Amora helped Angélica serve herself ice cream from the buffet. It's hard with just one hand. I'd never thought of that. Me neither, it just happens sometimes, and I don't know what to do, like doing up a zipper. Amora nodded. Opening it is easy, but it's sort of hard to close. I bet. Oh, I'm switching schools after the holiday. To mine? Yup! Wow, I can't believe it!

In that long academic year, their school won all six chess championships it signed up for. Their teacher was really pleased. Amora was really pleased. She and Angélica shared victories, chessboards, and headphones. During recess, as they lay under the trumpet tree, Amora held Angélica's imaginary hand. They both felt all those nameless things, all that inner shifting. Until Angélica said: Amora, I love you. Amora kept her eyes fixed ahead, glued to a spot where kids were mucking around on the playground. She rested her head on Angélica's shoulder and Angélica kissed her temple; it was a long kiss, full of warm thoughts. But later, what helped Amora make sense of everything was this corny sentiment, whispered in her ear: Amora, what a perfect name for you. You are made of love.

CATCH THE HEART RED-HANDED

She'd never had sex with a woman before and decided I'd be the one. The day it all happened, we met in front of the college building. She said she was tired of waiting and asked me why I never hit on her, if there was anything the matter. I said there was nothing at all the matter, I was actually super attracted to her, I just never thought she'd be interested, I didn't think anything of the sort was going on between us. I also said that at the party on the day we met, she hadn't seemed clearheaded, and seeing no interest on her part, I'd figured things would go no further. She got annoyed and accused me of being an idiot for not realizing how much she wanted me.

A college party where people ate hot dogs and drank lukewarm beer or wine out of plastic cups. Two months after class had started, and the university had decided to throw a shindig for people to mingle. About time. I'd been starting to feel weird about only seeing folks during the day—sober, drinking coffee, rushing to class. On the evening of the party, as was to be expected, there had been mayhem and boozing and heaps of embarrassments for the following days. Not on my part, of course, I've always been restrained. I spent the entire party hanging out in the same spot with Martinha. We'd only exchanged a few words until then, nothing of substance, though. After a few glasses of beer, things started flowing naturally, so of course I was totally content to spend the whole night right where I was, with her. Honestly, I don't remember anyone else from that night. I remember hearing someone cheated on someone else in the same bathroom where a third person later blew chunks. I remember chinked tiles and a loose hinge on the front door. I also remember a teacher trying to give a student a ride home at all costs. But my distraction-prone mind retained no names or details. Martinha had filled my eyes and my ears. Once I started mixing up words and struggling to stay upright, I suggested we leave. I put her in a cab and, since we lived in opposite directions, climbed into another one myself. I saw Martinha cup her mouth before giving the cabbie her address. I saw her turn around to look back at me, instead of looking straight ahead.

The night would've ended there if Martinha hadn't gotten out of her cab and rushed toward me seconds before I left. She let out a weird laugh and suggested we hit up another party. A friend's. She had promised to stop by and then forgotten about it, and now he wouldn't stop calling her. She insisted I come with her. I said all right and made her promise to remind me to call the cardiologist.

Earlier that day, when the nurse decided to take me to the emergency room and ordered an electrocardiogram, I saw Martinha's eyes saucer, and I'm sure she wondered what she was doing hanging out with this person—practically a stranger—who might die right then and there. I knew I was going to die, just not there, nor then. I was tired, though, and I must've looked awful, which I'm sure helped put the final touches on the scene forming in Martinha's mind. That morning, just before class, I'd felt terribly ill. I had an arrhythmia and had to go to the university hospital. Martinha didn't have a choice in the matter—our professor made her accompany me. I went into a room where the nurse asked me to lift up my shirt, take off my shoes, and roll down my pants. I knew the ritual. I'd had hundreds of electrocardiograms done before. I knew my heart had settled and that all I could do was wait and rest. She took the results to a doctor in the next room, then came to speak to me.

"Feeling better?"

"Yeah. See, I used to have WPW . . ."

"Aha, Wolff-Parkinson-White syndrome. But you're saying you used to have it . . . meaning you don't anymore?"

"No, I had a radiofrequency ablation done. Either it didn't work or there were other undiagnosed issues that are only now gracing me with their presence. Such as supraventricular arrhythmia."

"Hmmm, you're either the kind of person who likes to stay informed or a hypochondriac."

"A bit of both, I think."

"So do you often experience these tachycardias?"

"Not really. I had the surgery two years ago . . . the surgery, or procedure, or whatever it's called. I know I'm cured, or I was."

"Your electrocardiogram came back normal."

"I figured. You have to catch the heart red-handed to bring charges against it."

"Exactly."

"So what do I do?"

"We're going to keep you under observation for a few hours, and if you still look like you're doing well, you can leave."

"Okay, good . . . can I talk to my friend?"

"Of course, I'll ask them to call her in. Andressa will take you to the observation room."

"Right, thanks."

When Martinha saw me lying on the hospital bed, she pulled the most terrified expression I've ever seen. I told her I was fine and then filled her in on my history of heart problems and anxiety attacks. Another lie: when we arrived at the college party, she already knew a little about me because I figured it'd be a good way to wipe the fear off her face. So I told her about the day I was born. I told her I had taken the ambulance to Porto Alegre on my own and that my parents had followed. I told her I'd spent twenty days in the ICU with a catheter plugged into my head and that I suspected this was why my mom hadn't breastfed me and that this was why I didn't drink milk. Then I joked that maybe that was also why I was gay. When I said "gay," Martinha cocked an eyebrow like she hadn't expected me to slip that bit of information in with my heart problems and the story of my birth.

We spent the rest of the day together. Later that afternoon, she remembered the party. I didn't have much to do. Plus, I wanted to forget my shitty day in the hospital, to erase the scent of faux asepsis on my body. It seemed like a good idea. So we went. Everything was fine until we reached the second party.

She was standing by the balcony, drowsily watching the movement on the street below. The apartment was full. The party was thrown by a friend of a friend of a friend, and we were just two more bodies. We'd spent the day together, but there was still some of that awkwardness inherent to relationships that are neither opportunity nor friendship nor anything else, except a reprieve from unfamiliarity. We tried to divine each other's moods from afar. I felt almost detached, she probably even more so. Partway through our third glass each, she walked past me and wordlessly pulled me by the hand to one of the two bedrooms. She swiftly shut the door with my body and, with outstretched arms, encompassed me.

"I'd like to kiss you," she said, staring incisively into my silence and then turning her face toward the window.

"I'd like to, but I won't if you'd rather not."

"I can't see you."

"You don't have to."

She put her hand over my eyes and laid her hot mouth on my neck. "You smell exactly like I thought you would."

I couldn't speak. All I could think about was the filthiness of the hospital, the smell of coagulated blood mixing with that of rubbing alcohol. I thought of the greasy ER floor and the greenish chairs that so many bodies had sat on. She ran her tongue up the nape of my neck. I was paralyzed. Drawing away from me, she saw fear. She came closer, her hand still over my eyes, until our breaths were crisscrossing, until our lips were nearly touching, until the limits of latency. I gulped down air, and her breath weighed on my chest; between fingers, I saw her tongue run over anxious lips. A blast of warmth hit my teeth and tongue, and I retreated, bashing my head on the wood door. I affected nothing—neither embarrassment nor pain. A hand—half-cold, half-cutting—still rested over my reluctant eyes. She laughed quietly and made as if to run her hand down my face.

"No."

She stopped. She left her hand where it was and understood that there was some complicity between us. She carried on, frozen, breath willfully subjugated. I felt her cold hand beneath my shirt. My mouth parted slightly, my belly withdrew, and I let out a low moan, my voice a faint sliver. We tried to divine each other's moods from up close. She, malicious; me, passive. Her hand lingered over my uneven heartbeats, and my skin shivered.

"Is your heart all right?"

"Yes."

"It's beating super fast."

I laughed and reached out my hands, which had up to that moment hung limply at my sides, till they almost touched behind her, and I felt my legs quake.

Things ended there. Someone knocked on the door and we walked out of the room. Martinha was on my mind for days, the scene looping endlessly behind my eyelids and behind everything I saw—before bed, when I woke up, in the middle of the day, in line at the bank, at lunch.

The things I said about not realizing she was into me and that she said about me being a bit of an idiot were absolutely true. I apologized, claiming I was slow. We walked in silence down the hallway and into the bathroom. I splashed my face with water and left the faucet running, my gaze averted. I went into one of the stalls and she leaned on the sink for a moment before following. It was tight in there and we couldn't help but face each other.

I placed my hand on the back of her neck and pulled her toward me. We kissed. Only then did I realize how small Martinha was. I sat on the toilet and she straddled my legs. We carried on kissing, her legs relaxing over mine. I started unbuttoning her shirt and she pulled up her skirt. She tugged off my top and undid the clasps on my bra. Before I could react, she'd put her wet mouth to my breast. I threw my head back. The bathroom ceiling was incredibly tall. Martinha whispered that she wanted to be in a bed. The ceiling really was incredibly tall.

"But all we've got is this small bathroom stall."

I pressed my hand into her panties. She moved it away, out of shock, and undid me with one hand, awkwardly forcing her other down my pants and placing two fingers inside me. I closed my eyes. The noises around me became muddled.

"I'm not quite sure what to do."

"You're doing good."

She carried on. She bit my neck and breast while her fingers came and went clumsily. It wasn't her, it was everything. I felt her fingers grow tight inside me. Right then, I thought of my heart. Burning. I thought of all its mechanical flaws. I thought of the catheter plugged to my head, of the stench of piss in the bathroom, of the doctor's voice during diagnosis, of the mildewed ceiling. I thought of the valve inserted in my aorta, near my groin, so my blood wouldn't spill out during surgery, wouldn't gush out of my body. Red, hot, pulsing. While I grew cold, little by little dying. The blood draining away. I tried to deform these images, to force them out of my head, but failed. Me, growing pale and soft. She opened her mouth in shock and laughed unabashedly.

"I think I did it."

I cleared her smile with my mouth, breathed some of the life on my face, turned Martinha toward the door, and felt her sweat-slicked back on my chest. I tugged her panties to the side and slid my fingers inside her. One slowly, the other with more force. She threw her head back and let out a loud moan. I covered her mouth with the palm of my hand—for a moment, she'd forgotten we were in a bathroom. Martinha bit my hand, my neck, my hair, and my mouth, all the while moving her hips back and forth, pressing her hand over mine. There was silence. Then the cadenced shifting of her back, lower and lower. Her entire body lunged forward, and her hand slammed the blue wood door, which was when it occurred to me to lock it. She rose quickly. Not from shock but so that she could turn around and sit facing me again, damp. She rested her arms on my shoulders.

"You've got pretty breasts."

I didn't respond.

"A pity everything's such a mess on the inside."

She licked both fingers and, with them still in her mouth, looked deep into my eyes. We spent the rest of the day together.

GOD DELIVER ME

The hall was packed, and in the little room by the altar, Vera was getting ready for her first church sermon.

God deliver me from such a thing! I'm here by the grace of Jesus, hallelujah, and I'm so grateful. There's temptation everywhere, all around us, but I will not fall and neither will you. I am here, by the grace of our Lord, to testify that the blood of Jesus is powerful, oh yes, Jesus's blood is powerful! Our Lord came to me when I was least expecting it. He did not abandon me but instead looked after me and delivered me into the hands of an angel. An angel! And I flew, oh, did I fly, and I saw everything I had not seen until then, because I soared, way, way up high, hallelujah, and everything was so beautiful up there, off the ground, above trees and rooftops. From above, I saw a plaza and a church tower. Because I was way up high, clasping hands with my angel. The angel that God put in my path. Before then, my friend, I was in the dark. I was in darkness.

I'd walked aimlessly, here, on the ground, beside mundane things, beside all the things which we must love—for they are the Lord's handiwork—but which we must not welcome with haste—for they may be a trap laid by the Devil. And how are we to know? How are we to know? Why, by praying! By praying again and again and by asking God, Jesus, and the Holy Spirit to come to us in vision and to cast light on our tortuous paths. But our eyes adjust to darkness, and it is only once our legs have buckled under the weight of our bodies, the weight of our guilt and of our sins, that we realize we need help. I'd been living on the street. Homeless. Though my family loved me, they didn't know what to do with me, they didn't know what to do anymore. I was always high, always drunk, always in bed with a different man. And this is a small town, my friends, so of course everyone knew about it. This town's too small for so many men. You can frown all you want, I'm not scared of a frown! God is greater.

Hallelujah!

God has given me the opportunity to be here and to speak my faith because I believe in one true God, our Lord and Father.

And they joined in: All-Powerful, maker of heaven and earth, of all things visible and invisible.

Visible and invisible! Visible and invisible, my brothers! For He is the maker of all things. It was for us and for our salvation that He descended from the heavens. And He was incarnated by the Holy Spirit, in the bosom of the Virgin Mary. In His Mother's bosom, hallelujah! This is the point I wanted to get to, and this is where I will stop. Because after this there is only ruin. After the bosom came man. And then our Lord Jesus was crucified, killed, buried. The bosom is a symbol of faith, a symbol of love, a symbol of devotion, a symbol of care. Of course Jesus died for our sins, but dear friends, let us not forget that we may need a bosom to comfort us from time to time, to protect us like the Virgin protected Jesus.

And they nodded and threw their hands in the air.

Which is why I'd like everyone here today to know their angel, to learn to recognize them. Sometimes, they don't take the form we'd like. Sometimes, our angel comes dressed as a pauper, as a beggar. But we must learn how to recognize and love our angel and to respect their wishes. I met my angel on earth, the angel of light that the Lord sent me—praise be to God—to pull me from a life of damnation—a life of bottom-feeding and of filth—to free me of all that was evil. But I—I didn't want to accept it. I didn't! I was slow. Don't think it was easy. Not for me, nor for anyone around me. A change of life is no simple task. God tries and challenges us! And it is our responsibility to have the faith necessary to walk those tortuous paths, to see divine light in the most hidden of places. And you won't believe where God put my light. Would you like to know? Would you? Do you want to hear my story?

And in a chorus, they said: We do!

Well then. It was here, in this city, on a dark street, a street known to everyone as the destination of junkies, prostitutes, and inverts. I was there because that is where I went to waste my life away. Sitting on the sidewalk, I asked God to intervene, for I'd been robbed of strength. Leaning back on a cold wall, I smoked my last rock. Then things would go as they always did, with me dying a little. With me falling into a sluggish sleep so as not to feel the painful emptiness of life without faith. Not this time. No, instead, two arms lifted me from the damp ground and carried me to a place of comfort. If not God, dear friends, then I don't know who. In that moment, God sent down an angel, possibly my last. Next thing I knew, I was in a warm bed, my feet were clean, and I was fed tea and soup. I fought it. Oh, did I fight. For I didn't think I was deserving. But good things kept coming to me. I was offered a towel, a shower, a toothbrush, and when I stepped out of the bathroom, I did not recognize myself. I realized in that moment that I was still attractive. I was human. In that moment I found my voice, a voice that was thankful and gave thanks to real things. Yes! I gave thanks to the miracle, but also to *somebody*, my angel. My angel fed me, my angel cared for me, my angel gave me a home. I had a house, a house! Before then, I had never had a home nor a bosom. And why did I not have a home? Because I did not have love! And without love there is nothing. Nothing at all. Now, don't go thinking that it was easy to accept all of this—it wasn't. As I said, it came with a lot of prayer, not with a lot of speech. No! It was by meditating on the glory of our Lord that I came to understand, and when I surrendered, I did not fall but fly. Because the kind of love the angel had to give me was a love of surrender, a zealous love, empty of exploitation. My love was sincere. And it still is. I took my angel's hand so that I could face those things God had placed in my path. My angel's hands are soft yet strong. They caress me and hold me firmly so that I will not know falling. My angel gazes at me sweetly and gazes fiercely at the Devil's traps. And my angel has taught me to be at peace with God. And when would I ever have imagined that on that street—which was the only path I could see, my beginning and end—when would I ever have imagined that one of God's angels would come seek me there? But this is what my angel did! And my angel only did this because I asked. Hallelujah!

Hallelujah!

Which is why I've come to give my testimony of faith, today, before you, my community. My angel and I were married a month ago. Wrecked by drugs, my body can't bear children. But my angel already has a child, a child they have raised alone! God is wise and God is kind! I threw everything away and He gave everything back. This time, Father, I will not disappoint you!

And they pointed to the sky and repeated: She will not disappoint you, Father! We will not disappoint you!

Now, I want to call my angel to join me onstage to sing the Glory. Come on up, Leila!

For a few seconds, as Leila and Vera sang, Glory, glory hallelujah, glory, glory hallelujah, with closed eyes and upraised arms, no one seemed to understand what was happening. Little by little, the chorus thickened. Here and there, wavering voices joined worship. Until every voice rose in recognition of faith, because no one doubted the greatness of God.

THICK LEGS

It wasn't, it just couldn't be. Isadora had a boyfriend, didn't she? He was probably at that very moment sitting on the bleachers, waiting for her to come onto the field.

I'd always suspected the twins, Greice and Kelli, two stocky blondes with thighs wider than the entire breadth of my body. I don't know. Maybe it had something to do with how they walked, with how thick their legs were, but Isadora wasn't like that at all. Isadora came to practice with manicured nails. She had a *Malhação* notebook with Cláudio Heinrich on the cover, the height of heteronormativity. We were fourteen, fifteen years old and we all believed blindly in horoscope magazines. We were girls who did supposedly girl things. Was soccer a sign? I don't think so, nearly all the girls had boyfriends, except for Greice and Kelli, and I didn't have one because I was a *puta*, as they used to say, I hooked up with everybody.

The truth is I didn't even like soccer. I liked handball—or *ăndebóu* where I'm from—but stopped playing because some asshole kept calling me a lesbian, claiming I rubbed up against her during matches. On my mother's life, I was not a lesbian, and I wasn't attracted to her, either; she was way too ugly for my nonlesbian tastes. But Ariela, now she was really something. She used to fly into the zone, ball in hand. I'd watch her movements in slow, near-ethereal motion: Ariela with her long legs, bending as if in a classical ballet sauté, muscles tightening before expanding, flying, breaching the zone, her arm rising, veins popping in her fists as she bit her lower lip, then released the grip in her hand. A cannonball. Ariela was left handed, which confused people. On account of the ogre who was always calling me a lezzo, I became a goalkeeper to ward off any awkwardness. I was a great goalkeeper, a brilliant one. Except every time Ariela rushed toward me, everything disappeared, and I froze in her gaze. Marco, our after-school coach, always got really ticked off. He always put me up against Ariela because I was the best goalkeeper and she was the best wingman. I lost count of the balls I took to the face, the belly, I lost count of the broken fingers—but it was all worth it. At the end of practice, she'd hug me and tell me *good match, fair game.* Then she'd run her hand through my hair, plant a crackling kiss on my cheek, and bump me with a really lame punch. It became a sort of ritual for me, and if this didn't happen at the end of a match, it was neither good nor fair.

Oh, what I would've done to have arms like Ariela's! But mine have always been smooth, unblemished, and hairless, with no veins. Ariela's arms, meanwhile, were tan and dotted with freckles, her veins popped, and her knuckles were chunky from cracking them so often. My fingers are weird and all bent up these days from being broken so many times.

After the match, we'd sit on the bleachers with the boys. I was hooking up with Diogo at the time, a gangly German kid with a bowl cut. Ariela was hooking up with Felipe, a senior. We'd eat ice cream and then walk up to the park to watch the boys play basketball. My teenage years were chock full of sports and activities I wouldn't even dream of doing today. I don't know if the school encouraged us or if all the teens there just happened to like sports, but the fact is we always came out on top at the intramural tournament. We were hooked on games. I remember once cutting class with everyone to watch Grêmio and Ajax play the 1995 Intercontinental Cup. The *gremistas* suffered through the entire game, while the *colorados* spent the match rooting against every ball that entered the box. We lost in penalties. Four to three. The ogre who was always calling me a lezzie ratted on us to the guidance counselor, all because she hadn't been invited. The next day, everyone was in the principal's office, explaining themselves. Parents apologized to the principal and teachers and vowed it would never happen again.

The day after the event, Marco asked me if I wanted to play soccer. I said I'd rather watch soccer on TV, at home during class. He tried to feign annoyance, to act like he didn't agree with what we'd done, but instead he laughed at my joke. I said yeah, I'd like to play soccer, so he sent me to tryouts at a soccer club in the city starting a women's team. I showed up at the scheduled time and took the physical as well as an unbelievable written test on general and sports knowledge. The following day, he asked if I'd been selected as goalkeeper, and I said no. He pulled a saddish face, in solidarity, I think, and said maybe next time. Then I told him I'd gotten picked for offense. Jersey number nine. He looked at me, intrigued, and cracked a satisfied smile.

Isadora was number ten, Tui eight, and Rose eleven; Greice was five and Kelli was two, Simone was four and Jana was goal-keeper. I don't remember the rest of them. That was my soccer team. We traveled together and struck up friendships with girls on other regional teams. We had games almost every weekend. We were awful, but it didn't matter. It was cool to travel to a different city every Saturday and celebrate goals with pileups, hugs, or jumping around. There, I wasn't "a gross lesbian who rubs up against people"—there, I could touch people without fear of a stupid nickname.

A little while later, I bumped into some of the girls from the Parobé team at a gay party. Daphne Teco-Teco was shocked to see me. This was a long time after I'd stopped playing, about three or four years after, I think. She asked me what I was doing there and if I knew it was a gay party, and I said I knew, that was why I was there, so we laughed and she slapped me on the shoulder like she wanted an explanation. I just smiled and asked her to be patient, I didn't really feel like telling my story then. She pulled me up onto a small stage and said she wanted to introduce me to someone, her girlfriend. She looked over at the dance floor, then toward the room's darker corners, and pointed out a tall blonde leaning against the bar, her back to us. We jumped offstage holding hands. She dashed off, tugging me along, and introduced me to Sandra. I looked at Sandra, who nearly choked on her drink. She greeted me and said my name as she coughed with surprise. Sandra, the ogre who'd called me a lesbian at school. I laughed and said she should've paid closer attention to the hints she'd dropped me, and I swore I'd never, ever rubbed up against her in handball class. I wasn't even aware back then of my feelings for Ariela. Another day, I found Ariela on social media. She was a lawyer, married, with kids. No way, I thought. I thought of a bunch of things that day, the paths our lives had taken, then looked up the other girls on our team whose full names I still remembered. Apparently, I'd changed the least out of all of them. Might just be my impression, though.

I went to Isadora's profile and saw a bunch of photos of her and Kelli. They were married. So my eyes hadn't been playing tricks on me back then. Their passion for each other had always been there. I thought of the day I'd gone back for my shin guard. The whole team was warming up on the field, kicking a ball around. Except for Kelli and Isadora. Walking into the locker room, I heard the shower running. There were slats at the bottom of the stall door, and through them I glimpsed four legs in a tangle, a pair with rounded ankles that surely led to Kelli's thick thighs, and another pair with Isadora's manicured toes.

AUNTIES

They've been together since they were young. Aunt Leci was seventeen and Aunt Alvina fifteen when they went. It wasn't unusual for larger families to send one or two daughters to convent. They've been inseparable ever since. Sixty years. Does anyone understand what it means to live together for sixty years? I sure don't. After being in convent together for fifteen years, they decided to leave and bought a town house in the interior of Garibaldi, Rio Grande do Sul, where they began a new life together. Aunt Leci had a teaching degree and gave classes. Aunt Alvina was a spectacular cook. On their gate, they placed a small sign that said they sold cake, bread, and cookies. After a month of them being there, the line of people queuing for their delicacies reached around the corner.

My dad, Aunt Alvina's brother, was the first to visit them. Later, he took my mom and newborn brother. When I went to our aunties' house for the first time, the dust had settled, and everything had been acknowledged. Nobody discussed whether they should or shouldn't visit those two women who'd fled the convent to live together. No one else thought it strange, there was no reason to. I think things got better once everyone stopped asking questions. Time had passed. Aunt Leci and Aunt Alvina had settled down.

Theirs was a simple routine. They hardly ever went out. They saved their money for travel. It was their only indulgence, they said. On those trips, I think they got up to everything they usually couldn't. I mean, it's not that they couldn't do anything, I'm actually not sure, it's sort of unclear. All I know is they traveled a lot. The first time they announced they were going away, they telephoned my mom to ask if she'd look after Mitcho. My mom didn't really like cats, but she was so excited they were going traveling that she gladly accepted. Leci and Alvina were going to Italy. They were electric. The whole family was. Even Grandma, who had kind of stopped talking to them, went over to tell them she'd pray to Santos-Dumont to watch over their plane and not let anything bad happen while they were away. I think this was the first time anyone in our family had flown anywhere. They brought back gifts. Everyone got blessed rosary beads. And anyone who went to our aunties' house that month certainly heard them sing, *Volare ooo, cantare ooo-o.* A pity the photos fogged. Apparently, Aunt Leci dropped the camera, and none of the photos made it. It became routine, trips followed by the absence of photos. They got such a taste for traveling that they decided to go to a different country every two years. They visited Argentina, Australia, Austria, Chile, Colombia, Denmark, England, France, Hungary, Indonesia, Ireland, Israel, Italy, Japan, Madagascar, Portugal, Russia, Spain, Sweden, Switzerland, and the United States. They always listed them off in alphabetical order and laughed whenever they forgot one. It was all a game to them.

As years and the disapproval of certain relatives began to pass, Aunt Alvina decided to start hosting a family lunch at their house. Usually, family lunches were held at my grandma's, but Aunt Leci never liked going, she never felt comfortable. Everybody would ask about her. You see, she wasn't exactly family, though at home we always called her Tia despite her not being my dad's sister. After going to one of those lunches for the first time and hearing people gossiping about Aunt Leci, I understood why she felt uncomfortable. She knew those lunches and family get-togethers were important to Aunt Alvina. So in an attempt to please everyone, she suggested hosting one at their house. The backyard was big and had a meticulous garden, a lovely setting for lunch.

Aunt Leci went to town on the table arrangements and food, against Aunt Alvina's protests that the food was too much food and the decorations were too much, even though she knew they weren't, and everyone sang Aunt Leci's praises. In fact, talk of the two of them hushed whenever lunches were held there. The only thing you couldn't do was fawn over Aunt

Leci's dishes and not mention what Alvina had made—then you were just brewing trouble. At the end, they always laughed.

One day, I asked my mom if Aunt Leci had any parents or siblings. Her face dropped and she said Leci wasn't anyone's daughter—that she and Aunt Alvina had been living together ever since they met at convent. I didn't press her. Everything was clear, and more interesting than ever.

About three years ago, Aunt Alvina had a stroke and was in the hospital for a few days. Aunt Leci nearly died of sorrow. Tons of relatives arrived with offers to keep Alvina company and spend the night. Are you family? the receptionists would ask, and all the cousins, sisters, and nieces would nod yes. When someone's in the hospital, relatives come crawling out of the woodwork. But Leci wasn't a relative, and every time she came to stay, the receptionist would say there was someone in the room already, and relatives took priority on overnight stays. Aunt Leci would cry her way home. But what's your relationship to the patient, Dona Leci? the receptionist would ask. A friend, she'd say in a voice that craved sympathy. There's already a relative in the room, you can't go up right now. I think Aunt Leci only got to visit Aunt Alvina's room once, and she left with her heart in her throat. I drove Aunt Leci home, and she said: Family's everything at times like these, and we're lucky that Alvina's got family, we're real lucky, God is good, he knows what he's doing, everything'll be all right, she'll be home soon, I just have to look into getting some safety bars, the ones they put on the stairs, in the shower, in the bathroom, I'm not sure if Alvina will have any permanent damage. Tia, I know a physical therapist who does home visits, if you're interested. Oh, that would be lovely, my dear, yes, I'd like that very much, I think she might need one, right, a physical therapist to help in her recovery, but God willing, it won't be anything serious. Her mouth looks a bit droopy, don't you think, hon? Yes, Tia, but the doctor said it wasn't serious, Aunt Alvina's already talking, it's quite fortunate, isn't it? It is, sweetie, it really is, and what else did the doctor say, I wasn't allowed in her room for long—and her eyes filled with tears—what else did he say? He said it wasn't as serious as it could've been, but that she'll need physical therapy for her arm—it's been compromised—but that otherwise everything will be all right.

I started going to my aunties' house after the incident for two reasons: I wanted to help, and I wanted to understand how it all worked. In just a few weeks, I could tell they felt more comfortable. I'd spy one of their hands seeking out the other's as they hugged in front of the TV, and once I caught sight of a quick good-morning kiss in the kitchen.

On the day Aunt Leci caught a cold, Alvina was extremely nervous. She called and begged me to spend the night with them because she couldn't take very good care of Leci, who had a fever and wasn't speaking, in her condition. She begged me to please come by. Yes, that's sort of how the call went. I headed over. I'd never leave my aunties high and dry, especially now that I'd earned their trust.

They were dancing in the living room when I arrived. Leci didn't look particularly ill: Honey, we didn't call you over because I'm sick—it's just a little head cold, after all—but for your opinion, and for an explanation. Yes, an opinion and an explanation, Aunt Alvina echoed. I asked what it was and they told me without delay: We want to get married. It was so beautiful and unexpected I shed a tear. Leci continued. Everything we have is ours, it belongs to both of us, you know this. Except by law things don't work that way; if something were to happen to Alvina, God forbid, I'd be left with nothing, and what's more, if Alvina ends up in the hospital again, I'm not even allowed to look after her, I don't even have a right to visit her. You know how it is whenever an elderly family member is in the hospital: their room is crawling with relatives—they're like flies, Lord help us. Anyway, our question, dear, is whether you'd be willing to be our witness. It won't be a marriage so much as a stable union. We've already gathered everything we need, all we have to do now is pop by the registry office. Next week is a bank holiday and we're planning to go away on our honeymoon. And—we won't take no for an answer—we've bought you a ticket so you can come along, too. It isn't far, we're not going anywhere outrageous, just up to Maragogi. We'll have separate rooms, of course. Are you in? Wait, don't say anything just yet. First, picture having to worry about other things on top of the sorrow of loss, picture me having to leave my house because it isn't exactly mine. Picture Alvina not getting a pension if I die—we're living off my retirement now. Picture all that and then think: we're two old ladies, and what do people usually do with old folk, they chuck them here and there, like bags of rubbish, and honey, we really are quite the handful. So what I'm saying is, isn't it best this way? They'd thought of everything. All I had to do was say yes.

They were married, and they carried on as happily as ever. And that's how things will continue, till death—or some bureaucratic red tape—does them part. In any case, theirs remains the best and most successful marriage in the family.

BITE YOUR TONGUE

When her mouth was already full of blood, she decided to go to the bathroom to check on it. Before, they'd been fighting. Their eighth fight that weekend. In this latest, they'd discussed never having time together and how they should organize themselves accordingly. This had spilled over into how unhappy she was that year, how her friends thought she was a joke and there wasn't a thing she could do about it, except, that was . . . and she bit her tongue so hard she immediately forgot what she'd been saying. She screwed her eyes shut as the other person waited for her to end her sentence. All for nothing. She gripped the tablecloth, balled up her hand into a fist. She finished swallowing the morsel of meat, which tasted raw despite being overdone. She sat frozen in her chair, eyes fixed on a grease stain on the tablecloth. The stain bothered her; the tablecloth shouldn't be stained, not in a place like that. Manuela asked what was going on because her silence had become too long. With her hand splayed on her forehead, she rambled that she had bitten her tongue, then thought of what dreadfully inconvenient thing she had been about to say that had made her bite down with such force. Her mother had once said that people hurt themselves unconsciously when they were doing something wrong. Maybe she was unhappy with her relationship, or with herself. Maybe she should never open her mouth, because everything that came out of it was a lie. Maybe she didn't want to pass the time or travel or buy an apartment or any of that. And now there she was going on and on about things she didn't want. All to hide the obvious: she'd cheated. "Fuck," she said, her tongue swimming in saliva and blood. The stain was still there. She got up and walked to the restroom.

Facing the mirror, the sink spattered red, she tried to recover the line of reasoning that'd led her to conclude she was a fraud. A personal failing. Why was she lying so outrageously? It was too great a leap. If only she could have an insight or two during her pricey sessions with the psychiatrist, things might be better, she might be able to unravel her thinking until she found a plausible explanation for herself. But there were no plausible explanations. Of course it was at a restaurant—where people took in more than they put out—that she would find an explanation. She lifted her head to face the mirror, noted that she looked a little pale, but blamed it on the white fluorescent bulbs across the ceiling. Before checking her tongue, she bared her teeth, like a person studying their ferocity. She wanted to leave—not just the restaurant but her unhappiness. There. It wasn't just Manuela but everything that held her back: forced happiness, plans, the desire for children. None of it appealed to her. She wanted to run in the opposite direction, to flee, to cower, but without losing her stable, monotonous, happy life in exchange. She opened her mouth again, still brimming with blood. Enough to frighten a mother and her small child as they left one of the stalls, but not enough for them to ask if everything was okay. She smiled sardonically with her blood-stained lips and gave them a wide berth. She felt a little light headed and took a seat on one of the toilets. Someone outside asked if she was okay. It was Manuela. She said yes and saw that she was having less trouble speaking, probably because she'd spat out all the blood starting to pool in her mouth again. The bathroom empty again, she went back to the mirror. She stuck her tongue out. She must've bitten down with huge force—the thing was deformed, purplish. A small section had been gnawed, right at the tip. She closed her eyes, felt droplets of sweat gathering at her temples and a sense of imminent collapse. Opening her eyes, she saw Manuela's reflection in the mirror.

"What's going on, *amor*?"

She leaned on the doorframe and slid into the stall. Sounds became muted in her head and everything blurred. Someone asked her to reiterate how she was doing. She felt like crying. She rested her head on the cold tile floor. The memory of the man invaded her. She faced the wooden door but searched for a window. The flirting, the consensual pursuit to the park, a body pressing her against a tree, tacky goatee, thick hands squeezing her breasts, hard cock rubbing against her roughly, wet pants, going down, cock in mouth, his cock in her mouth, him coming. With more breath than voice, she said that she was fine and asked Manuela to head back to the table and eat without her. Manuela insisted she at least drink some water. Reaching her hand out of the stall, she grabbed the bottle and, without opening her eyes, shoved the bottle neck in her mouth and drank. She gulped down all the blood. She heard Manuela leave the bathroom. She took another sip and left some of the water in her mouth. She remembered the taste of his semen, the stain on her pants. She'd felt good, grimy. She saw blood in the bottle as she opened her eyes; it drifted slowly, poetically. As a spectacle, it would've been lovely to watch the red stain dissipate into the clear water. But it was no more than blood floating about in a bottle of water. There was no excuse for what she'd done. It hadn't been love, it hadn't even been interest. Just a desire to know another body.

Her continued absence annoyed Manuela, who sat on her own. The food was only half-eaten but most of her hunger was gone. She set down her knife and fork, diagonally. The soda was getting warm, and the waiters had started circling the table, gesturing at the people waiting in line. Manuela got up so others could sit. At the same time, as if aware that everyone was waiting for them to leave, the other woman came out of the bathroom, looking pale. There was still blood in the corner of her mouth.

Manuela and the woman walked to the register, their backs to the table. The waiters immediately swept away the dishes and set the table for a family of four: father, mother, children. The woman remembered leaving her coat draped on the back of her chair and circled back. She asked for her coat, looking squarely at the man. She searched for the stain, but they had changed the tablecloth.

WASSERKUR, OR A COUPLE OF REASONS NOT TO HATE RAINY DAYS

Were there reasons, I'd start by saying I hate rainy days, but I won't. Rainy days leave me so sad I don't even have the strength to hate. All I want to do is write. No, not want, but need. But some days, like today, I find myself islanded somewhere far away from home, from my computer, my writing things, unable to reach my notebook or any inspiration. And I realize that I'm at a bus station, at a bus stop, with soaking feet, the street's flooded, and I'm contemplating everything I would do if I weren't wet. Yet without the rain, I wouldn't have this urgent need to write. Then I become even sadder as I hear the civil defense force discussing floods, rescues, and landslides on the radio: families who've lost all of the little they had, babies almost drowned in their own rooms, the elderly swept away by currents as they slept, and all those other calamities that go hand in hand with downpours, all told in a newscaster's dramatic, articulate voice. Today, I am at the Porto Alegre bus station. You'll understand the chaos implied by that circumstance. I'm islanded. The average delay is three hours. The streets are flooded, and there are intermittent closures. The bus station's greasy television screen has just reported that the Porto Alegre–Canoas highway is partially flooded. Meaning I won't be home anytime soon. Which is why, right this moment, I'm not sure there's anything to like about rainy days. Except I wouldn't want to say I hate them, either.

I don't like the sound of rain when I'm standing in it, and I don't like cheap umbrellas; they're insincere, and they bust at the first gust of wind that whips around the corner. I don't like to see trash amassing on the sidewalks and in gutters, don't like people who walk with open umbrellas under the awnings— they might consider leaving room for someone without one— don't like cars that don't yield to drenched pedestrians, and I don't like the smell of people, either, especially smokers; the stench of cigarettes grows sharp in the humidity. I hate the smell of cigarettes, but more than that I hate the smell of wet cigarettes. I had a friend who always showed up at college in the morning with freshly washed hair and smelling of smoke. Every time she moved, a sweetish, slightly sour, dirtyish cloud would radiate toward me permeated with that awful stench of cigarettes and hair conditioner.

Today is especially sad because morning came without the promise of sunshine. You know when you look outside and you're clear on the weather's limitations, convinced the sky won't shower you with blues and golds, certain the only color you'll see is gray? Well, that's today. Still, I always try to fool myself by thinking of good things, of dry socks, lunches, and trashy TV. I've had two coffees and was blown off twice today, and it was all the rain's fault. Just like it's the rain's fault that all the buses I could've taken home are parked at gate three, with no sign of leaving. Looks like I'll be here for more than three hours.

I pen these humid grievances into the margins of my journal.

On rainy days like these, everything inside and around me becomes messy, which I find difficult, being of a naturally sad disposition. What I mean is that I'm not cheerful. Sure, I may be funny, but that's different. Even when I'm warm and dry, I'm always in that melancholic sort of mood they say is better suited to rainy weather, and maybe that's why I dislike rain so much, on account of the intensification. In any case, it's hard for me to quell the tears that well up in me. They're quiet. Instead of running down to the bottom of my chin, they sit still, around my eyelids, brimming at the edges. Some drip down corners or advance down my cheeks, but they always dry out before tracing that last curve. They don't flow like real tears. From the outside, my sadness seems muted. The gristle of my disillusionment stays on the inside and carves a melancholic force in my heart, which I try to cover up with more lies. Maybe I shouldn't have put it quite so simply, in such an orderly way, but that's how it is. Everything my eyes see becomes blotchy, like a lens that tries to soften reality but instead of realizing any fantasies simply blurs it. As I said, on rainy days like these, everything inside and around me becomes messy. Maybe I'll give you this journal, maybe I'll trash it, maybe I'll use it to fashion a boat and send it down-gutter until it clogs up a sewer.

You told me that on rainy days you can neither read nor drink coffee, and I'd add to that that you also can't smoke cigarettes or wait on chance encounters. On rainy days, I exist because I can't not. I don't want to die on a rainy day. I can't die on every rainy day and only come back on dry ones, with feet that are always warm. So instead, I dream.

I dream that, on rainy days, you watch the shapes drawn by the classroom parquet and hear the professor's distant monotone. I dream that you want to be submerged, immersed in one of the puddles that form torrentially outside, or maybe in a thick rectangle of rain that falls from a single fat cloud, a *tromba d'água*. I dream that the professor lectures us on *Wasserkur*. Distracted by the windowpane, you miss the end of his sentence and yet still know that it was about art and transience. You think. You don't exist. I dream you are talking about teeth and about walls.

When I am far from you, I feel sad, and even though today we are close, I still feel sad. I don't know if this is the rain's fault, too. It must be. For a moment, though, I imagine that you made it rain for our date. I really am untrusting. Even more so when I'm tired or when I have a headache; maybe this is the source of my pessimism and distrustfulness. It's just that I spent all night awake wondering if we'd see each other again, and I felt this urge to see you because I like you, as if you had been part of me for a long time. And what I'm concerned with is creating love in the space of this distance, which, today, the rain has kept from shrinking. I look down at the bus station's muddied floor, oblivious to how I'm meant to do this. I know these things happen, maybe they're already happening. I don't want to shield you from anything, but I don't want anything bad to happen to your teeth, which are like walls put up in the wrong place. It's just that I know how, on rainy days, and within our minuscule field of vision, we sometimes come up against obstacles—be it a hole, a wall, or a will-not-attend.

It's just that this rain is getting in the way of my urgency. Funny, isn't it? Without rain, there'd be neither urgency nor this intensified sadness. Therein lies the paradox: rain impedes the thing it fosters.

More than a dry and quiet place, what I'd like is to sink my feet in water, maybe because I just remembered what the professor said, in his monotonous voice, about it being a cure. About how placing your feet in water can heal anxiety, cold, nostalgia.

Tomorrow will be December, then it'll be a new year, then in September it will rain again, and I will be alone. I feel like sinking into water to cure myself of the love I don't have and to keep from feeling nostalgic for something that doesn't exist.

Which is why I give up on leaving. I'm going to fashion a boat from this journal and then use some more pages to make a jacket. I'll buy cigarettes to smoke under the awning and blow fumes at people in a rush. I'll get my socks soaking wet so that later I can look down at my feet and see that they're white and withered. I'll come up with reasons to love and hate the rain and to love and hate this day and, maybe, to hate you, too. Until I find you at the café you go to on every rainy day so no one will see you reading or drinking white coffee, because then they'd know you'd lied when you said you didn't do these things on rainy days. And I will unmask you.

AUNT BETTY

First, Marcos's laughter rang out, then mine, followed by a feeling of utter stupidity, senses seized by laughter that simply pushed the air further and further out of the body. One of my hands gripped the casket while the other covered my face and mouth, as I tried to fake tears that convinced no one. Everybody could see our laughter bursting out, until Marcos—in that backstep where air noisily recoiled through nose and throat—grabbed my arm and we sank beneath the coffin. My mother became a demon. I tried to plead forgiveness with my lips, but she burned my soul to a crisp. The rest of our relatives glanced at each other in confusion. A dozen or so old biddies sitting in a row made the sign of the cross with their soft hands, a silent quaking chorus, from foreheads to chests to shoulders to foreheads to chests to shoulders, kissing their rosary beads at the end. The only person who remained undaunted was Aunt Betty, who resembled a grand old lady in her casket. An adorable woman lying there among flowers, surrounded by family and friends, peacefully rising above and, in our memories, already metamorphosing from Bitter Betty into a beloved aunt. Death has a way of lending people a benevolent air. Marcos and I knew otherwise. We laughed not out of spite but precisely because we remembered how nasty she was. *Nasty* was Aunt Betty's favorite adjective. In her eyes, everybody was nasty: Mário's daughter was a nasty girl! Tônia's niece is so nasty. José, what a nasty old man. All nasty Nora's husband can do is be nasty. It'd become a running joke, and we teased out its variations.

Aunt Betty always had opinions about everything and everyone. Usually, none of them positive. Marcos, who was gay, knew all about this and was fortunate enough to have moved to the United States, which meant he didn't have to show his face at parties or family events as often as I did. Hence his immunity to everyone's remarks. He was always talking to me about how important it was to say no, to guiltlessly bow out of things, but I couldn't. I wasn't aloof, I tolerated interactions. Our family adored get-togethers: weddings, christenings, gigantic, indigestible lunches where relatives I'd never seen before and would fortunately never see again sprang up all over the place like rabbits. Aunt Betty had loved these gatherings more than anyone because they presented opportunities for her to needle at some dark secret in all of us. Not anymore, though.

Some time passed before we were scolded. About two minutes, I think, two slow minutes of us laughing like prostrate pigs under metallic struts that drew beautiful arabesques on the pedestal. It occurred to me at some point in the middle of all this that I'd never seen the bottom of a casket. My dad was the one who yanked me up by the arm and berated me with spittle and gritted teeth. Daniela, what kind of forty-year-old woman splits her sides laughing at her *tia*'s funeral? I stopped. Not because of the scolding but because of the number—forty—echoing in my head. I was a forty-year-old woman, among many other things.

To my dad, I was a good daughter, albeit an unfortunate one. "A pity you never got married for real." To my mom, I was "a terrible daughter, a black sheep—and single to boot—all you do is bring me shame." To Aunt Betty, I was "a luckless, cancerous girl with a dried-up uterus who brought her parents nothing but grief, a poor, pathetic creature." But I *had* been married, to Tereza, for eight years, and I'd been single for two. As far as my dad was concerned, it hadn't been a real marriage but a phase. A phase that'd been going strong for twenty-two years. My mom pretended that she knew nothing, heard nothing, and had never seen a thing, and she was always, always asking when I'd get married and get my life on track. She forced me to go on dates with the sons of her work colleagues and, until recently, hosted awkward dinners to which she invited these same work colleagues' sons and, midconversation, offered me up like discount-shelf merch. The guys, of course, hit the ground running. For my part, I made no effort to be agreeable, all of which my mom would later throw in my face in the shape of a nervous breakdown.

The worst was during the novena. Before it began, my mother and her church group would get together to decide what to pray for. Generic prayers went unheeded, so my mom prayed for me. Virgin Mary, please let my daughter Daniela meet a man who's patient and puts up with her temper, a man who is good and quiet and rich. It tickled me that Mom was always burdening the poor Virgin with that task. What tickled me less was that she'd talk to a murderer before she'd talk to Tereza.

Aunt Betty developed a twisted sort of sympathy for me after Marcos, Tereza, and I paid her a visit. Though we were cousins, Marcos was the brother I'd never had. We'd grown up together and together discovered how life worked. On one of the few occasions Marcos was in Brazil, we decided to spend a weekend in the countryside, and my mother suggested we visit our aunt. We acquiesced. Tereza and Marcos went as boyfriend and girlfriend, and I went as myself, except with uterine cancer. As usual, Aunt Betty served us her famous, brick-hard home-made cookies and lukewarm coffee that smelled several days old. Tereza excused herself to go to the bathroom. And that's when Aunt Betty let it rip. Your girlfriend's a bit dark, isn't she, Marcos? Yes, Tia, she's black. Marcos, how dare you! Don't you say something like that about the nice lady, she's so polite! She's just tan is all. And Marcos went to town. No, Tia, she's black. Shhhhh. And in walked Tereza, who'd heard us from the hallway and was trying to hide her laughter. We kept on chatting, Aunt Betty seemed really animated. Then it was my turn to leave. I went out for a cigarette, but I said I wanted to see the dogs to avoid a lecture. And when's Daniela going to get married, huh? They're saying she's a—and she pointed both hands at her feet and marked a large space between them. When's she going to get engaged? You should talk to her, Marcos, she respects you. Soon, she won't be able to have kids anymore. No one'll want her . . . Which is when Marcos dropped the bomb. Tia! For the love of God, don't mention children. Dani had uterine cancer! Cancer? God have mercy! The poor girl. And Marcos continued. She's dried up, Tia, there isn't a man who'll take her. Sweet Jesus! She's cancerous, then? Marcos said Aunt Betty's face dropped so hard it nearly fell to pieces. I'd taken a lap around the house and was eavesdropping through the window. I wasted a couple of drags from my cigarette giggling at Marcos. I would've smoked another fifty, but I didn't think it fair to leave them alone with her for so long. When Marcos's turn came to leave, Aunt Betty was quiet. She seemed like she wanted to say something to me, she even had a tic in her eye, but in the end she kept mum. Of course, that same week she called my mom to ask about Marcos's marriage and my cancer. Quickly grasping what was going on, Mom came up with an excuse to end the conversation. Then she called me and, in a tone that sounded like she was on the verge of disowning me, said: What've you done? You're heartless monsters! I will *not* lie to your *tia* for you! Except she did end up lying, because to her the stories of Marcos's marriage and my cancer were far more palatable than my fucking a black woman and Marcos being an ass bandit.

Five years of lying passed before Betty died. No one expected it, not even her. Uncle Olímpio, her brother, witnessed everything. She'd been doing really well, you know? She'd gone to clear some leaves from the gutter that morning. I said I'd do it in the afternoon, *chê*, but she isn't one to wait, is she? I wasn't ready, *chê*. I still haven't gotten used to the idea. But Olímpio, I'm sure she went peacefully, I'm sure she's in a better place now, my dad said. Peacefully, *chê*? Aunt Betty screamed blue murder before she keeled over. She knocked over dishes, buckets, she howled, *I'm dying and the sink is full of thawing meat!* I told her to simmer down and sit for a while, that it was just the heat and the strain from climbing onto the roof, *chê*, but the woman would *not* sit still and kept letting out these terrified yelps. Then she went cross-eyed, slammed her hands on the table and on her chest, and fell face-first into a cheese platter. Oh my God, Olímpio, is that what happened? I wouldn't wish that sort of death on anyone, or for anybody to witness such despair. And then she left, *chê*. Fucking hell, and the meat just sat there in the sink, didn't it, I can't even imagine what the stench must be like now. Sure, but don't you worry, we'll go over later to help you clean up. My dad squeezed my arm as I tried to contain my laughter.

Another large gathering at Aunt Betty's: thirty or so people floating between reminiscence and commiseration. The stench of meat had soaked through the entire house, but no one seemed to care or want to comment. It was like Aunt Betty was still there, making remarks that would've left the same funk in the air: about my singledom; Marcos's inability to hold down a woman; Olímpio, who didn't have a place to lay his head and had to move in with his sister; my dad's spinelessness; Sandra, who was never home to look after her kid, which was why her husband had found somebody else; Igor, who was cockeyed, a thing no one tried to fix—that's how it would've gone. None of us were talking about any of it, though, and we were like strangers to each other. We knew all of these things, but insofar as we kept family matters and issues clammed up, we seemed to turn into a group of strangers brought together by someone's passing. A certain disquiet settled into the house, a nausea. Maybe it was the smell of rotting meat, maybe it was the driving force of change and everything that came with it. I looked at my uncles, my aunts, and my cousins, their faces dipping behind cups of tea, behind the steam from hot cups of coffee and cigarette smoke. All of them blank. I walked to the window, where my great-aunt Otília was sitting. I petted her arm gently. She was devastated; she and Aunt Betty had been close. I squatted down by her armchair, which was squarish and made of yellowed leather, and propped both elbows on the hard armrest. Aunt Otília gave me the most forlorn look in the world. I looked around and saw everyone was grieving my aunt, and I felt ashamed for laughing. Something had to be done. It was for the good of the family, to breathe new life into our get-togethers and build new memories. It was the first time I ever felt my family splitting at the seams. This sense of nonbelonging hurt. I bent over to kiss Aunt Otília, pressing my lips against her bony old-lady cheek, and, as I retreated, whispered in her ear: Did you know Marcos is a fag? Aunt Otília's eyes brimmed with life. I drew away from the armchair, emanating compassion, and went out for a smoke. My aunt got up to get some tea and pulled my mom and two cousins to a corner of the hallway. Ten minutes later, everything was as before. Faces became familiar again, and heated issues made the rounds; there were wrinkled noses, warm looks, muffled laughter. There, there. Everything was as it should be.

FAREWELL INVENTORY:
A STORY IN FOUR DISTANCES

First Distance

I have known you ever since the world was the distance that separated us but never kept us from meeting. I have known you forever, since the first fear of meeting you. I have known you before desire. I have known you in the unknown of strangers. And since then, the desire to touch things, intimate, incorporeal, and ephemeral, at all hours has begun—because though they may finish, they do not end. I have known you from inside desire. I have known you as surely as a missed beat in an unfinished movement. I have known you since the feeling of warmth in my chest, chill in my belly, bother in my plexus, since throat stumbles and knotted feet. I have known you from the edge of harsh conversation and of mornings over bedsheets. I have known you feeling whole and frightened. I have known you in tears and in pleasure. And in tears again. And in tongue and speech and moan. I have known you bleary eyed, ever since the world was the rustle of your eyelashes. And I have known you ever since the world was the urge to leave. And I have known you ever since the world was a tactile, tempestuous, yet forgettable *saudade*. And I have known you ever since the world. And I have known you wanting. And I have known you. And I have.

Second Distance

To take inventory. To list details. To quantify love as hours. To account for occurrences. To describe assets—which you gave me. To ritualize the imperative distance taking, from the beginning that is known, from the beginning expressed as the end. The end. The. To describe, because love is not the right label but an intrusive word that, at three a.m., colonizes every phrase.

Inventory:
> Two empty cups on the side table
> Some hair
> A striped T-shirt
> A white T-shirt
> A green toothbrush on the sink
> Broken sunglasses
> A business card from L'Armagnac Café
> Our scent
> A mirrorless mirror frame

Third Distance

Two empty glasses on the bedside table are enough to create the body's chaos. The other day, the glasses were full. And they served to dampen affections. Today they are washed, emptied, see-through, disguised. Yet in that time-place-movement—which always eludes you and eludes me—they remain full. They hold mineral sensations and images captured at the cusp of dream and desire. On the bedsheets is the time March stole from February, the sleep morning returns to the eyes, the quiet morning returns to the eyelashes, and the weight morning returns to the body. Time: recommended movement between legs and restless feet; ribbon of saliva between mouth and mirror image; the vowels of foreign words in my heart. My body is dressed in the only sense of touch that still holds some part of your physical presence. And I wonder if it still belongs to me, as if there were any sense in being clean when our memories have been forgotten. There are places that exist so that we may revisit memories in temples and so that we may say that there really are temples that hold memories.

Fourth Distance

If all that exists were stripped away. Only the echo would remain.

Listen from the precipice.

Listen to everything said in a rush.

Listen to everything impossible to say.

Pause.

Long pause.

Theatrical pause for the theatrical.

I invent you.

Sugar-free.

I say farewell.
Sugar-free.

And swear it is all substance-truth.

SHORT & TART

MOLOTOV

A pity. A real pity the meeting happened so late, late at night. Glasses already empty and heads already full, a pity. The rise and fall of notes of no consequence, or better yet, of consequences that would be tragic were they not pathetic. Those nymphs, those muses, those minds—I twist my fingers and sigh, thinking of the Molotov cocktail that came at me like a good-night kiss. Next thing I knew, the bottle had burst and the room was ablaze—flames flickered between us—and I felt shards of glass slicing my face. I open my mouth to breathe, shards in my mouth, I chew. Hot glass. Hurt lips, teeth, tongue. My mouth fills with blood, I swallow everything. Bits of teeth, tongue, lips, glass, and fire, and with my fingertips I reach for you. You're burning. Your skin smolders and your hair takes on the blackness of coal before it becomes ember.

You are immobile, impassive, impenetrable. A deaf man smiles and reaches his hand toward me and, being deaf, is unmoved by the roaring fire, or by any of those things that to me seem shrill. The man hugs me, I shake loose and rush toward you, embracing your abrasive body, which blisters me. My body hurts all over. I am flesh, I am living.

YAWN

I want to see you tomorrow, and contrary to what people might think, it won't be too late. Honestly, it'll be perfect. Tomorrow, everything will be quieter and I'll have had a decent lunch. You'll have slept in, and you will wear a sleepy expression, as if you've slept a good, dream-filled sleep. We'll be good. You'll be in those dirty sneakers and I'll be in an old pair of jeans and a shirt I love that's a little bit torn, and you'll poke fun at me. With a sly look in your eyes you'll tell me I should dress better now that I'm thirty. I'll pinch my lips and glance at you out of the corner of my eye until you start laughing and saying I should give you the shirt. A drowsy yawn will cut through the irony and through any belabored thoughts. The wine you have will be white, while I will drink cantaloupe juice. I'm sure there'll be laughter; cantaloupe juice is odd and doesn't taste like much. I'll tell you about how ever since I was ill and spent a month eating only cantaloupes, I've been hooked on them.

You'll say I must be high on cantaloupes, which might very well be true. Then I will feel a pain on my left side, right beneath my ribs, which I'll quickly forget. You'll worry and say it's all right, you'll take care of me. I'll sigh and you'll take a glug of your wine, and then you'll lick your lips and the few droplets that're still clinging to them. But before they've all gone, I'll cover your lips with mine, and with eyes shut, we'll think life is good. Because tomorrow will still be summer.

SALIVA

Sometimes I get this urge not to write. This urge not to pour myself into words or into the twisted meanings of sins or shins. And I resent papers and pencils, and sometimes even keyboards. And not even sugar can remedy this disgust . . . not even guidelines, topics, or obituaries. It's the kind of thing that leaves your lips pursed as if poised to whistle, protruding in anticipation of syllable or sibilant. And I think: Go on! even if it comes from my mouth, since my fingers have frozen and my head just dances and dances and doesn't right itself, aligning the faults and filling the flaws. The worst part of all this is that everything stays at the level of the skin, of the hair, of a nervous acidity, to the side, at the back of the mouth. But it's all just wind, desire, saliva.

FISTS

Full of small poems, my hands closed into fists. I couldn't bear the metaphors being crushed, struggling to survive. They slipped away from me like granules, granulated poems. I closed my fists as hard as I could and still they trickled away. My arms were heavy, my shoulders, my back, and all the blood built up in my once-fine veins.

I wanted to clasp her fine white neck and crush it with all the verbs she never used. To drown her and, maybe, draw out all the things I wanted to hear and that she never thought of saying. All the things that were actually only mine.

It was my hand that rose and punched me. Again and again until my nose was gushing blood. Until my face was disfigured. And when I could no longer recognize myself, I kept on punching and punching to see whether I felt anything, any kind of contact, any kind of strong and passionate caress. Even pain, even anything that made me feel—as I'd heard said—alive. But

I felt nothing. There was no space left to fill inside; I was full up. Full of words, all of which were your name.

My tired body, crammed with your empty name and with a ridiculous urge to laugh, to expel the air between one void and another, until there really was nothing left—neither membrane nor plasma nor air.

WALTZ

You're strange sometimes, she said, as every head turned to look somewhere else. Mine watched the fire dancing in my belly die out. I felt like saying that sometimes I really was a stranger, but more to myself than to her. I felt like saying that I couldn't recognize myself when my intensity was restricted to my heart, which led to those arrhythmias. One, two, defect, one, two, defect. My mouth opened in a response that never came. It stayed in there—where answers are written—without contours or fillings. All just air shuddering between pelvis and neck. It had been sweeter in the beginning, near the plexus. But then it spread across my skin and hardened, pressing veins against muscle and bone until, finally, it left me—then returned in one, two, defect, one two defect cardioelectrophysiological.

SLEEP

I think the only reason I get through the night is the coffee on the other side, at the brighter end of those nighttime hours. It's always the same: I lie down—half lie down, actually, my back leans against the wall—sometimes I turn on the TV, others I just lie there and grow sleepy and soft, then roll over onto my side, facing the window, and later onto my belly with my head facing the opposite direction. And I fall asleep. My sleep probably lasts an hour. I wake up religiously early every morning, so I try to get to bed early too. So by the time the clock strikes ten, I'm lying down. Then cue the process just described. While sleeping, though this isn't always the case, I am beset by the strangest dreams in which children are dogs, or vice versa, and are bewitched by beasts that become violent whenever they see anything French, erotic, or green. These dreams take place in old houses. Sometimes I recognize them, sometimes I don't.

My friends are always in a hurry, and I feel distressed. Anyway, all sorts of images mix, such as incandescent globes, tiaras, and demolition machines, and I feel like I'm going mad, then wake up. I awake in the darkness of dawn. That's when I think of the morning and of the coffee I will drink when the sun starts affecting the night. Which is to say that, to me, coffee's more than just nutritional; it's built on the fantasy of dawn, a new light that stands in opposition to night, suffering, and darkness.

All that said, I should clarify something. I don't always suffer from insomnia or night terrors, like I said before. If that were the case, my life would be hell. Usually, I sleep well. I'm only struck by the frightful agony of sleeplessness when I'm on my own. Just me and my demons.

That was a difficult night. I spent hours half lying and watching TV before finally deciding it was time to sleep. I got up haltingly, I'd been considering it for a while, so I did. I put a few droplets of sleep tonic into a glass with a little bit of water. I'd bought the vial three years earlier, and it was still half-full. I don't really like taking medication. I don't take illegal drugs. Sometimes I drink. I smoke. I drink coffee. Just as I was starting to feel the usual mellowness of opiates, I thought of how it had been a long time since I'd taken any. I stumbled into the bathroom and saw that the medication had expired. Which was all I needed to spiral into despair. But the sluggishness was greater. I couldn't wake my mind, which just laughed. And mocked. And sang of consciousness to come as if it were singing of death. And there I was, desperately trying to stay awake. But before I knew it, I was swimming with demons.

STRANGE

strange, adj. and n. 1 of something peculiar, extraordinary 2 belonging to another place, foreign 3 unfamiliar, new 4 that which breaks away from social standards 5 that which is not a part of something 6 mysterious, enigmatic 7 that which avoids interactions

1. She was ugly. No, you couldn't say her beauty was wild or exotic. She really was ugly. Extraordinarily ugly. The kind of person you really have to look at when you look at them, but without disclosing the indecency of your scrutiny. The kind of woman at whom children saucer their eyes and drop their jaws, then ask their mothers if she is a witch.

2. She arrived, confident, stared the clerk squarely in the eyes, and said, *Messiê, sivuplê, ú é la garr du norr?* The man smiled and said, *Just arraund ze corrnêrr.* Her smile fell to pieces with her French.

3. How bizarre of everyone to wear those hideous sneakers that looked like dress shoes but were neither one thing nor the other. She was happy she'd gone barefoot. But everyone thought it odd.

4. A rebel teenager without a cause in torn jeans struggled to grasp that what she really needed to get that funk off her was a shower. She could even go on wearing the same clothes.

5. She tried to make friends. At home, alone, she felt like part of the group.

6. She wrote the letter and, before posting it, set it on fire.

7. She couldn't cross the line. She gave up on that point.

MEMORY

I no longer remember her voice, nor what she called me early in the morning. I no longer remember the way her hands slid down my back, nor where they ended up. I no longer remember the smell of her. I don't remember how my hands buried themselves in her hair, nor her frightened look whenever I talked about us. I remember neither old things nor those one might consider recent. I don't remember whether her feet were ugly or small. I don't remember whether she had a big mouth. I don't remember if she spoke softly. I don't remember if she liked bergamot or if she liked to watch TV before bed. I don't remember whether she spoke another language. I don't remember whether she liked dogs or if she had a cat. I don't remember what her hair was like when wet. I no longer remember how she used to write. I no longer remember the books she wanted to read, nor the ones she had already read. I don't remember if she walked normally or listed to one side. I don't remember if she did the dishes properly. I don't know if she liked pop art. I don't know if she traveled to Europe or if she went to Japan. I don't remember if she liked trains. I don't know if she played the guitar or the piano—or neither. I no longer remember whether her skin was smooth. I don't know if she played with dolls or if she walked on stilts. I don't know if she ate sand and I don't remember either if she ever complained about the food. I don't remember if she liked white or black or orange, or if she had ever watched *A Clockwork Orange*. I don't know if her hands were warm or her nails manicured. I don't know if she skated or rode horses. I don't know if she had a mom or a dad or an older sibling. I don't remember if she had relatives. I don't remember if on Fridays she drank Brazilian limeade, sweetened with condensed milk, or if she liked to start the weekend off with guava mimosas. I don't remember if she had an affair, or a house, whether she bought a bicycle or asked for my hand in marriage. I don't remember if she complained about having to separate the trash from the recycling or if she was an activist aggressively opposed to PET bottles; it's possible she composted in our apartment, but I can't remember. I don't remember if she hung art around the house or if she didn't care about the blinds' peeling brown paint. I don't remember if she had a high-pitched voice or if she liked Carmen Miranda. I don't remember if she wore lipstick, if she bought makeup from catalogs or at the drugstore. I don't remember if she hated calendars or if she liked to turn things in late. I don't remember her shoulders, or her hair, or the shape of her breasts, I don't remember her breath or if she drooled on her pillow. I don't remember if she wore flip-flops. I don't remember her leaving. I don't remember if she forgot her keys. I don't remember if she took her books. I don't remember if she washed the dishes, broke plates, soiled her blouse, or if one day she walked right into a door. I don't remember the size of her, how tall she was, how much she weighed, or if I felt safe when she hugged me. I don't remember a thing, not the texture of her lips, whether they cracked in winter or were sunburnt in summer. All I have left is a photo. And I don't remember where I put it.

FAILURE

She smokes; she thinks and smokes a cigarette while pieces of paper and dishes pile up on the table. She taps ash into a mug. The dregs of chamomile tea, days-old saliva, and now ash mix in the yellow bottom. She thinks. The open window welcomes in a gust of wind that makes the crumbs dance on the plate and then scatter, sticking to the pages of books, pages that are no longer smooth. There's nothing to hide. There are no secrets or desire, which is why there are no adequate words. Intentions wither in trial. Voided. There can't possibly be anything worse than an original no, she thinks, fashioning a new failure.

Absent.

She realizes: the truth of a no, the original negation, the one that unwarrants the act, the one that stops things while they're still in the planning stage, a knife and its abrasion, shredded needlework, pallid urges. She is another shirked beginning, a building site undug, a place where purpose lacks foundation; they're fantasies, she knows, pillars of smoke on which to balance her goals, her lenses.

The shrewdness of the magician who has lost his gift.

Exhaustion.

She loses control of her eyelids, loses control of her steps, her sense of direction, and yet carries on, she can't not, the weight of her body propelling her onward, like a zombie—only her back is automated—unknowing, she goes. She collides with a horizontal plane, a red line that edges the junction of what, in the end, is blue.

She looks out the window, the gust, the mug, the backyard, the crumbs, the books, the ground, the ground. She plants her two fearful, pained palms—she knows she is supported—forges a tangent, lifts off. Her hair hurts. She knows she can try. She can always try.

TEMPLE

I kicked a stone down rue du Temple. She asked why I was always kicking things. I said nothing, just looked squarely ahead, like someone who wanted to keep on. I kicked the entire temple. Everything before me and around me crumbled. The sounds of what we one day discover and desire to be. Nothing is solid now, not the sidewalk, not the eroding buildings. Not even time, much less so-called time. *Construct* is an unsightly, truncated word made to be knocked down. She was still looking at me, waiting for me to provide a logical explanation for a nasty habit: kicking. The two of us stood on a street corner knowing that Paris no longer wanted us, Paris didn't even know who we were.

PROFANATION

Come, blanket me with your hair and let your citrusy perfume linger on me for hours; come wake me up—grouchy and frisky—and run your nails, your hair, your mouth along my entire body; walk through my chaotic house and break my old flowerless vase—a reminder that spring will soon come again, because life is inescapable, cyclical—and turn on the burner till we've been intoxicated by leaking gas. Switch on the light. Explode me into a thousand pieces; dash through the hallways bashing into door handles; talk to the neighbors, clog the keyholes with notes and chewed-up gum, tell the super I died and come to my window to serenade me with the tackiest songs you can think of—it isn't late, but too early to keep on sleeping—bring the coral sun and all the morning's smells into our room and stain my sheets blue with dreams and nightmares; let your hand freeze over my chest in winter and put on yesterday's David Bowie tunes. Dance. On the table—because I don't have any lunch engagements—balance my plates, swallow my knives, bend my spoons—you've got a gift for magic—but don't vanish; you mustn't saw me in two, but you can mess with my heart, turn on the fan and blow me to bits—just don't start at the neck because that's just so, so clichéd—blow on my feet, between my toes, my shins, I might just grow wings. Leave so that you can call me at dawn singing *la canción más hermosa del mundo*, the loveliest song in the world, and burst into laughter during the second stanza, because I love to hear you cracking up, I like it when your eyes tear up from laughing too hard; so come back here laughing, come back laughing, clumsy, drunk. No. You can stop. Ever since you showed up, I haven't known who I am or who you are anymore; except I remember, I stress, I pause to think, because you're so much more than all I've ever had. Cut my hair, wax me, wash my skin—I promise to drink only water for a week—do you think there's a problem? I want to do things right this time and not leave room for fate to thieve my joy. I'll walk to the corner with eyes shut, counting backward until I reach your phone number, until I reach the day we met for the first time—because I still want to get to know you, every day. I want to know what you like so that I can challenge you and because that cheeky expression you make when someone can't grasp the obvious is so charming. I just want us to understand one another, even if it's complicated—because you're so free—you're your own mistress—while I'm so strict and regimented; but I have subtracted and divided our loves so that I know how much we can love one another in one day, so that we needn't worry about imminent misfortunes and instead can plan trips—because I want to go traveling with you—crawl into my suitcase or take my hand, and let's cross the street, the river, the world; run the globe with me, let's leap across continents; let your hair grow long again—I like it when it billows—then cut it again to upset me. For my part, I will try to remain unchanged so that you will always love me. Oh, so you like surprises? Well, in that case I'll switch things up. But would you mind explaining how I'm meant to do that; it's hard, after so much planning and counting, to leave the beaten path and attempt an unchoreographed dance. I don't know how to paint. The only thing I know how to do is write the same text I've given you every single one of the 1,825 days we've been together. Is that too long? Don't tell me I'm wrong, that I can't count to save my life; I need explanations to survive, and if I can't believe every day that I love you for being who you are, I risk no longer feeling a thing. Is that the sort of risk you want to take? I didn't know. Sorry. Everything becomes profane.

ABOUT THE AUTHOR

Photo © 2018 Laine Barcarol

Natalia Borges Polesso is from Bento Gonçalves in Brazil. She is a writer and a translator with a PhD in literary theory. She is the author of *Cutouts for Photo Album without People* (2013), *Amora* (2015)—which in 2016 won the Prêmio Jabuti, the Jabuti Amazon Reader's Choice Award, the Book of the Year AGES Award, and the Prêmio Açorianos de Literatura—and *Control* (2019), among other titles. In 2017, she was one of only two Brazilian authors on the Bogotá39 list, which selects the most promising Latin American authors under thirty-nine.

ABOUT THE TRANSLATOR

Photo © 2016 Dagan Farancz

Julia Sanches is a translator of Portuguese, Spanish, French, and Catalan. She has translated works by Susana Moreira Marques, Noemi Jaffe, Daniel Galera, and Geovani Martins, among others. Her shorter translations have appeared in various magazines and periodicals, including *Words without Borders*, *Granta*, *Tin House*, and *Guernica*.